SPY KIDS™ ADVENTURES
A NEW KIND OF SUPER SPY

Written by Elizabeth Lenhard

Based on the characters
by Robert Rodriguez

VOLO

HYPERION
MIRAMAX BOOKS
New York

Printed in the United States of America

First Edition

1 3 5 7 9 10 8 6 4 2

This book is set in 13/17 New Baskerville.

ISBN 0-7868-1716-X

Visit www.spykids.com

Carmen and Juni Cortez were having an ordinary evening at home. Ordinary, that is, if you're a Spy Kid.

They were in the basement training room of their cliff-top mansion—locked in combat. At the moment, Carmen had the upper hand.

Literally.

She was hanging by her knees from a trapeze that swung from the training room's ceiling. She swooped toward her brother from above, aiming her boxing glove right at his head. Juni's red curls sproinged wildly out of his big, padded headgear, making him look like a goofy Martian.

And an easy target.

Boink!

Carmen's boxing glove connected with Juni's poofy head, sending him tumbling to the exercise mat on the floor.

This was not a surprise to Juni. Carmen was the

best boxer in the Spy Kid division of the OSS. (That was the top-secret government agency where the kids, and their parents, were spies.) So, before he and Carmen had begun sparring, Juni had slipped a secret weapon into his pocket. Now, its moment had arrived!

Juni reached into the pocket and pulled out a small purple bottle.

"Uncle Machete," Juni whispered to the bottle, "please, don't fail me now."

Uncle Machete was Dad's brother and a great gadget inventor. Well, *usually* great. With Uncle Machete's inventions, you never knew what you were going to get—edible parachutes that tasted like liverwurst, perhaps. Or intelligence software that spoke to you only in Swahili.

The Machete-made gadget Juni was counting on at the moment was Glubbles—glue and soap bubbles, all in one.

Well, Juni thought, taking a deep breath, here goes!

He pulled a circular wand out of the bottle and expertly blew a giant bubble. As it shimmered and bobbled up into the air, Juni slapped his hands onto it.

And it worked! Juni's hands were stuck fast to

the bubble. When the glimmering orb rose silently toward the ceiling, so did Juni.

He looked down at his sister. Yes! She hadn't seen a thing. Assuming that Juni was still sprawled on the floor, she was swinging idly on the trapeze. Finally, she did a lazy triple somersault into the air and landed gracefully on the exercise mat.

Pop!

Yup—that was the bubble going kablooey.

"Aaaaaaahhhh!"

And *that* was Juni plummeting to the padded floor. Carmen glanced up and squealed—right before Juni's boxing glove bopped her on the head with a *boink.*

"Urgh," Carmen whimpered. She toppled over. Juni made a crash landing next to her. They lay side by side for a moment. Then, woozily, Carmen turned her head to glare at her brother. Crashing to the ground from the fourteen-foot ceiling might have taken Juni down, but he was not out. In fact, he was grinning smugly at Carmen.

"New gadget?" she accused. "No fair."

"A good spy always has a surprise in his pocket," Juni replied with a grin. He stood up and ripped open the Velcro wristbands of his boxing gloves with his teeth. He pulled the puffy gloves off and pulled a chocolate bar out of another pocket in his cargo pants.

"Gee, *winning* that fight sure made me hungry," he announced. He ripped open the chewy snack. As he gnawed on the candy, he gazed down at Carmen.

"So . . ." Juni said smugly. "I just won a sparring match with the famous Carmen Cortez. I wonder what the other kids at the OSS would say if they knew you were bonked into oblivion by your brother. Your *younger* brother."

"Don't you breathe a word," Carmen hissed at Juni as she pulled off her own boxing gloves. "You just got lucky. That doesn't mean anything."

"Maybe I should let everyone at OSS HQ know," Juni said.

Carmen definitely didn't want that. After all, Carmen was twelve and Juni was only ten. She'd be humiliated.

"Please," Carmen pleaded. Then, as Juni crossed his arms over his chest and got an even more scheming look in his green eyes, her voice turned even more imploring. "Please?"

"What's it worth to ya?" Juni asked.

"Name your terms," Carmen shot back, sticking her chin out.

"I get to choose the family pet."

Carmen glared at Juni. For the past month, the two had been arguing about their ideal pet. The arguments went something like this:

"How about . . . a garter snake?" Juni would say.

"Uh-uh," Carmen would reply. "Puppy."

"You know I'm allergic to anything furry," Juni would say. "How about . . . Japanese stag beetles?"

"Puppy," Carmen would retort.

"Cockatiels? African naked mole rats? Buenos Aires tetra fish?!"

"Puppy."

To say the spy siblings did not agree would be an understatement. But finally—Juni had some leverage. Carmen would have to agree to a non-puppy pet now!

"Okay," Carmen agreed, slyly. She turned on her heel and walked over to the backpack she'd stashed in the corner. She pulled out a well-worn library book about animal breeds. She flipped through its pages for a few minutes before she declared, "You can choose—between a yellow Lab or an Irish setter."

"Carmen!" Juni complained. "You know if I so much as sniff a schnauzer, I start sniffling. And sneezing. And scratching."

"And that's a problem?" Carmen said innocently.

"Uch!" Juni huffed in frustration.

"Okay, okay," Carmen said. "You might as well tell me your latest idea."

"Frogs!" Juni announced. "They're very cool. We could start them off as tadpoles. And we could breed flies to feed 'em. And—"

"And *gross*!" Carmen said, sticking out her tongue. "A frog is something that sleeps in the bottom of a pond, not at the foot of your bed. A puppy, on the other hand . . ."

"Is entirely out of the question," said a Spanish-accented voice behind Carmen. The Spy Kids spun around and found themselves gazing up at their father. He'd just emerged from the flight-and-fight simulator. This was an enormous, gunmetal-gray contraption stashed in a corner of the training room. OSS spies used the simulator to learn how to duke it out on the wings of flying airplanes.

Dad pulled off his virtual-reality goggles and shook his head at Carmen.

"Done sparring already?" Juni said, smiling up at his dad. Of course Dad was on his side. The Cortez men had to stick together!

"Who won the fight?" Carmen asked.

"I did," said a scratchy voice behind their dad.

That was Mom, hopping lightly out of the simulator. She walked over to her family, fluffing her ginger-colored curls and grinning.

"Yes, it is true," Dad said with a shrug. "Your mother wins every time. It is because I let her."

"*Really*, Gregorio?" Mom said. Then she reached out and grabbed Dad's elbow. With a simple twist of her index finger, she sent him into a double front flip. He landed on his back with a thud.

"Oof!" Dad grunted. Then he gaped up at his wife. "Ingrid, I was just joking!"

"So was I," Mom said with smile. Then she reached down to help Dad to his feet. "I didn't hurt you, did I, honey?"

"No, no," Dad said with a little moan. Then he looked at Carmen and Juni. "Your mother is a very clever woman, kids. Do not mess with her!"

"Believe me, Dad," Juni said, "we know."

Once upon a time, Carmen and Juni had thought their parents were kind of nerdy. They'd worked at home as consultants. Dad wore wire-rimmed glasses. Mom did laundry. Carmen and Juni couldn't have imagined their parents arguing over a parking space, much less beating up villains.

But then, the kids had discovered that their

parents were spies, and there was little they *weren't* capable of. Of course, that didn't mean they were perfect. In fact, when Mom and Dad had gotten into a major jam on one of their missions, it was Carmen and Juni who'd saved them. That's when they had become Spy Kids.

Now the whole family fought evil together.

And *that's* why Dad was dead set against a pet.

"Now, children," Dad said, dusting off his training fatigues. "Who's going to take care of a frog, or a dog, while we are off saving the world? I ask you."

"One of the household robots?" Juni suggested. "They could take care of my frogs, easy!"

"Give it up, Juni," Carmen said. "All a frog's gonna do for you is make your warts come back."

"It's toads that give you warts, puppy breath," Juni said.

Carmen glared at her brother and turned to face her parents.

"Please, can we get a puppy?" she begged. "We could keep it outside."

"No," Mom said. "You know Juni's allergies are too sensitive for that, Carmen."

"So . . . we'll keep Juni outside!" Carmen said desperately.

"No!" Mom and Dad blurted together. "Case closed."

Suddenly, the training room lights turned red and started flashing. An alarm began blaring through the house.

"That's the OSS!" Juni said.

CHAPTER 2

The Cortezes scrambled upstairs to the kitchen and positioned themselves in front of the microwave oven. When Carmen tapped a few buttons, the microwave door converted into a plasma computer screen. And onto that screen flashed a face—it was Devlin, their boss at the OSS. His cleft chin was stony, and his brown eyes were grim.

"Hello, Cortezes, thanks for the quick response," he said. "Ingrid, Gregorio, you're needed in Brazil, ASAP."

"And us, Mr. Devlin?" Carmen asked respectfully.

"Well, Carmen," Devlin replied, "I need you and your brother to hold down the pen . . . er, I mean, fort."

Carmen and Juni exchanged glances.

"Devlin, I am sorry," Dad said to the screen. "But we Cortezes, we usually work as a team."

"And a great one at that," Devlin said. "But on

this mission, Spy Kids would stick out like a clean spot on a pig."

Juni couldn't help but giggle.

"What's the mission, Devlin?" Mom asked.

"It requires two adults with a terrific tango, a stellar salsa, a magnificent meringue," Devlin said. "Think you can handle it?"

"I am a Spaniard, not to mention a suave spy," Dad said, puffing his chest out just a bit as he addressed the microwave. "But of course!"

"Then here's the scoop," Devlin said, folding his hands on his desk. "There's a dancing school in Rio de Janeiro called the Cha-Cha-Cha Academy. The place seems to have a strange effect on its students."

"Strange effect?" Juni asked.

"Yes," Devlin said. As he nodded, he made a little snorting sound with his nose. "It seems that students enter the Cha-Cha-Cha Academy looking to brush up on their, well, cha-cha. But they emerge as stealthy—and very flexible—criminals. Then they slink around the city through the sewers. They slither into jewelry stores and insinuate themselves into people's homes. Then they grab everything they can get their slimy hands on.

"Yes, and the National Bank of Brazil appears to

be the next target," Devlin went on to say. "Which means, Ingrid and Gregorio—you'd better strap on your dancing shoes and get ready to rumba!"

Early the next morning, Carmen lolled on her parents' bed while her mom packed up her spy bag with gadgets and weapons. Mom also tossed in a personal cell phone.

"Remember, Carmen," she said, "this phone has a protected frequency. If you and Juni need to reach us for any reason, just call us!"

"What would we need?" Carmen said sulkily. "Help with math homework? After all, Juni and I won't be on a spy mission."

"Is that what's bothering you?" Mom said.

"I just can't believe you and Dad are going off on a mission by yourselves," Carmen complained. "It's not like the OSS to split up the Cortezes."

"I know, honey, but you know what you always say," Mom said. "'You can't send an adult to do a kid's job.' Well, sometimes, I guess it's the other way around."

"Well, that kinda stinks," Carmen said.

"Carmen," Mom said, sitting on the bed. "You can't go on *every* mission. But it doesn't mean you're not a spectacular spy. I'll prove it to you."

Mom strode across the bedroom to her vanity table. Then she hit a button next to the mirror. With a whirring noise, the mirror slid to the side, revealing the family safe. Keying a combination into the digital lock, Mom opened the safe and pulled out a small box. She returned to the bed and handed it to her daughter.

"What's this?" Carmen asked quietly.

"Something I think you're ready to have," Mom replied.

Carmen opened the box and gasped.

"An OSS bracelet," Carmen said. "It's identical to yours!"

Carmen had always loved Mom's glinting silver link bracelet with the moonstone charm. The stone was set in a silver circle engraved with the letters OSS.

"You have an OSS ID card and an OSS code name," Mom said. "But *this* bracelet makes you truly an elite spy—a woman spy."

"You're saying we're cooler than Dad and Juni?" Carmen said incredulously.

"Not cooler," Mom said with one of her signature warm smiles. "Just . . . different."

"Thanks, Mom!" Carmen said, wrapping her arms around her mom's slender shoulders. "I'll wear it all the time, just like you do."

"That was the idea," Mom said with a grin. As she clasped the bracelet around Carmen's wrist, her own moonstone sparkled in the light. "Wearing this will remind you that we mother spies and daughter spies have to stick together!"

"Even if we're *not* on the same mission," Carmen said with a shrug.

"Speaking of which, I'd better finish packing." Mom slid off the bed and went to the closet. She rifled through her disguises and pulled out a slinky dress covered in red fringe. Then she grabbed a long-stemmed, silk rose off a shelf, along with a pair of high-heeled dancing shoes.

"Ah, the tango," Mom said, tossing the clothes into her spy bag. "That's our favorite dance, your father's and mine. Why do you think we named you Carmen!"

Carmen felt herself blush. Were *everybody's* parents this mushy? Time for a subject change.

"So, who's staying with us while you're gone?" Carmen asked. "Uncle Machete?"

"No," came Dad's voice from the doorway. Carmen turned to see Dad striding into the bedroom, shaking his head. "Machete says he's too caught up in the Jumping Jack Flash to spend the weekend with his niece and nephew. My brother—

always with his head in the clouds."

"Dad, you've got to admit," Carmen said, "the Jumping Jack Flash *does* need major work. My test drive of the prototype vehicle last week was a disaster!"

Carmen flopped back on the bed. It made her feel queasy even *remembering* that ride. The Jumping Jack Flash, or JJF, was perfectly round and made of superbouncy material. It was launched by a spring button just like the kind in a pinball machine, except it was much, much bigger. The JJF traveled by bouncing hundreds of feet into the air over and over. And over. And *over*!

"It would have been okay, if it had bounced in one direction!" Carmen said. "Or if it didn't flip over and over when it bounced. Or—"

"If it didn't have such a dorky name," Juni said. He'd just popped his head through Mom and Dad's bedroom door. "Jumping Jack Flash? What's that about?"

"It's Machete's and my favorite song!" Dad said, sounding wounded. "You know—by the Rolling Stones."

"Rolling Stones?" Juni whispered to Carmen with a giggle. "Talk about ancient."

Then he turned back to Dad.

"Anyway, if Uncle Machete isn't staying with us, who is?"

"Well, that is a problem," Dad said. "My mother, as you know, lives in Spain. Uncle Felix is not really your uncle. And your mother's parents—well, they're on a spy mission of their own, it seems!"

"Guess we'll have to turn to our *other* family," Mom said. "The OSS."

Mom went to her makeup table, which doubled as a computer terminal. After she tapped a few eye shadows, her makeup tray flipped over. On its underbelly was a glowing keyboard. Mom typed an instant message to Devlin.

And only a few seconds later, she looked up from her vanity mirror/computer screen in surprise.

"It's like Devlin read our minds," she said. "Looks like he's already arranged for two new OSS agents to come stay with Carmen and Juni. Their names are Octavian Buss and Kitty Lieder. They're already on their way over."

Dingdong!

"That must be them!" Carmen said.

CHAPTER 3

With Juni jostling behind her, Carmen opened the front door. She found herself gazing up at a tall, sinuous woman wearing leopard-print leggings, a fuzzy black sweater, and lots of black makeup around her almond-shaped eyes. She blinked at Carmen lazily.

"Carmen Cortez, I presume?" she said.

"That's me," Carmen said. "You must be Agent Lieder."

"Please, call me Kitty," the woman said. When she shook Carmen's hand, one of her long, sharp nails left a red scratch on Carmen's wrist.

"Oh, I'm sorry!" Kitty cried. "I really should trim down my 'claws' here." She waggled her long, red-painted nails at Carmen playfully.

"Um, sure," Carmen said as the woman slunk into the foyer. Kitty stopped in front of Juni and bent over to look him in the eyes.

"And you're Juni," she purred. "I recognize you

from your picture on the 'Spy of the Year' plaque at the OSS."

"Aw, shucks," Juni said, blushing a little. Then he blushed a lot! And then, he *sneezed*—all over Agent Lieder's face!

The woman sprang away from Juni and hissed in disgust.

"Sorry, Kitty," Juni said, rubbing his nose, which was feeling sort of sniffly all of a sudden.

"Maybe you should take something for that cold, Juni," the woman replied.

"I didn't think I had one," Juni said, shrugging. Then he looked around. "By the way, wasn't another agent supposed to come over with you?"

Kitty glanced around the foyer. Then she shook her head in annoyance.

"Oh, Octavian!" she said, slinking back to the front door. "He's so shy. Always hiding. Of course, that does make him an excellent spy."

Kitty opened the front door and called, "Octavian!" A very tall, very bald man with downcast eyes stepped into the foyer. He extended a long, skinny arm to each of the Spy Kids.

"Octavian Buss," he said curtly. "Hello."

Then he ducked into a shadow against the foyer wall and clammed up once again.

"Oh-kay," Carmen muttered. "*This* is going to be interesting."

Before she could further scope out the sitters, Mom and Dad bustled into the foyer with their packed spy bags. No sooner had they introduced themselves to the new agents than Kitty all but shoved the Cortez adults out the door.

"Well, hello and good-bye," she said in her rumbly, purring voice. "Off to Rio with you. You don't want to miss your flight."

"True," Mom said, "but call us if you need—"

"We'll be just fine," Kitty interrupted. "Shoo, shoo!"

"All right," Dad said as he and Mom stepped through the front door. "And the emergency numbers are on the refri—"

"Bye, bye!" Kitty said. Then she slammed the door in their faces and whirled around to face the Spy Kids.

"Okay, kittens!" she said. "First on our agenda— new gadgets!"

Carmen blinked in surprise.

Juni sneezed again.

And then, wonder of wonders, Octavian spoke up.

"To go with the new gadgets," he said, looking

shyly at his long, skinny feet as he spoke, "we'll teach you a new form of martial arts. It's called Mon Kae Si, Mon Kae Du. It was created by Himalayan monks just for the OSS."

Juni turned to Carmen again and whispered, "And I thought staying home from a mission was going to be boring!"

Boring, no.

Exhausting? Absolutely. Over the next six hours, Kitty and Octavian ran Carmen and Juni through a marathon of training events in the basement. They stocked their spy bags with new gadgets. They spent hours Mon Kae Si–ing and Mon Kae Du–ing. And all the while, Juni sneezed and sniffled.

Finally, everyone ran out of steam. The sitters left the training room to hit the showers, while Carmen and Juni sprawled on the exercise mats, staring at the ceiling with glazed eyes. They were wiped, but happy.

At least—Juni was. After a five-minute rest, he got up and gathered up his gizmos. He could barely decide which to play with first.

"I haven't gotten this many new gadgets since Uncle Machete had that garage sale!" he said. Finally, he settled on the Holo-Goon. Seizing the ray-gun-shaped, lime-green device, Juni flipped a few switches, then pulled the trigger. A three-dimensional cartoon monster sprang out of the Holo-Goon's muzzle. The creature was purple and squat, with a big, jiggly belly and warty lumps on its head. It stuck its tongue out at Juni and made a rude noise. Then the creature did a little dance. Finally, the monster burst into a cloud of neon-green dust.

"Completely cool," Juni breathed.

Carmen just looked at the poof of dust skeptically. "Juni, have you noticed something about these gadgets?" Carmen said.

But Juni wasn't listening. Instead, he'd dropped the Holo-Goon and began flapping his arms up and down. He held his breath until his eyes bulged. Then he gasped for air and whispered, "This one is from the Mon Kae Si, Mon Kae Du. Octavian taught it to me. It's an ancient and mystical martial arts move."

"Uh-huh," Carmen said dryly. "And tell me, Juni, what does this ancient, mystical martial arts move *do*?"

Juni's arms stopped flapping.

And his eyes stopped bulging.

"Well, it, um," Juni stuttered, "it . . . uh. . ."

"And what's up with that Holo-Goon gadget?"

Carmen said. "It has a lot of bells and whistles. But where's the umph?"

"What are you saying, Carmen?" Juni said. He glared at his sister.

"I'm saying," Carmen said, flopping back on the exercise mat. "I think our baby-sitters just spent six hours wasting our time. If you ask me, a good karate chop blows Mon Kae Si, Mon Kae Du away."

"Oh, yeah?" Juni challenged. "Care to make it interesting? Let's spar!"

He launched himself into another Mon Kae Si pose. This one involved a handstand and reciting the Pledge of Allegiance, backward.

Carmen rolled her eyes and got to her feet. She eyed Juni as he executed a wobbly handstand.

"One nation," Juni began muttering, "indivisible . . ."

"*Hai!*" Carmen barked. Her flat hand shot out in a single, precise, lightning-fast karate chop. She only tapped Juni in the knees. But that was enough to send her unbalanced brother flying across the room.

"*Aaaaigggh!*" Juni cried as he landed on the exercise mat with a thud.

"The only reason I'll forgive you for that," he

grunted, "is because you seem to have knocked my sneezes out of me."

"*And* because I've proved my point," Carmen said. Her brown eyes turned serious. "Something's odd about those agents, Juni. I think we should investi—"

"Dinner!" Kitty called from the top of the basement stairs. "I'm not much of a cook, so I thought we'd just have Fooglie Puff cereal and PB & J. And for dessert, an ice-cream sundae bar. Plus, Octavian brought his killer DVD collection over."

"Excellent," Juni said. He hopped to his feet and dusted off his training fatigues. Without giving Carmen another glance, he dashed up the stairs.

Carmen rolled her eyes.

"Silly gadgets and cereal for dinner," she muttered as she crossed to the stairwell herself. "These are the weirdest baby-sitters ever. But—they seem harmless enough. And movies and a sundae bar? I can think of worse ways to spend an evening!"

CHAPTER 4

"**U**rrrrrgggh," Juni groaned. It was the middle of the night, and he was supposed to be asleep. But he wasn't asleep. He was bent over in his bed, clutching his stomach.

"Okay," he whispered with a wince, "maybe eating two butterscotch-cookie-dough banana splits wasn't such a smart way to spend an evening."

He flopped his arm up onto his pillow and glanced at his spy watch. The spy watch was a satellite communication system, a mapping locator, a cell phone, computer, *and* countless other gizmos, all in one. He and Carmen never took them off their wrists. Which meant Juni only had to glance at his wrist to see that it was 4:17 A.M.

"Urgh," he moaned again.

Juni looked at his personal robot—Ralph the Second. The buglike silver critter was curled up in the corner in "sleep" mode. If Mom and Dad were here, Juni would have sent Ralph the Second to their room to wake them up. His mom would have brought him some flat ginger ale to settle his stomach. Then she would have put her cool hand on Juni's forehead and smiled at him comfortingly. And before Juni knew it, he would have been drifting off to sleep.

Juni tried to imagine Kitty Lieder getting him ginger ale and putting her hand on his forehead. But all he could picture was a big bowl of Fooglie Puffs and Kitty's long, spiky red nails.

"Ugh," he shuddered. "I think I'll fly this mission solo."

He lurched out of bed and padded downstairs to get his own ginger ale. But as he approached the kitchen, he heard a sound.

A lot of sounds, actually—the rattling of pots and pans. The crashing of the garbage can tipping over. The tinkling of breaking glass.

Someone had invaded the Cortez mansion!

Juni dropped to a crouch and began creeping down the dark hallway. He wished he had his night-vision goggles. Or a weapon. Or his sister. But there was no time to gear up. First he had to figure out what he was fighting against.

Pressing himself flat against the wall, Juni tiptoed toward the kitchen door. When he reached the door, he got into fighting stance.

Meow!

Juni blinked.

Meow? he thought. My big, scary intruder is . . . a cat?

Juni rolled his eyes, untensed his fight-ready muscles, and walked into the kitchen.

I wonder how a stray cat got into our house? he thought. I'll get the broom-bot to hustle it out of here.

He looked around for the mystery guest.

Where'd it go? he wondered.

Finally, he saw a shadow scurry across the far end of the kitchen. A very large shadow.

Juni froze.

Then he dropped to the floor and started sweating.

That kitty cat was—Kitty Lieder!

From what Juni had seen, the Spy Kids' baby-sitter was still tall with two hands and two feet. But, in a few very scary ways—she'd changed. Twitchy whiskers had sprouted from her cheeks. Her eyes had gone green and glowy. Her ears—fuzzy and pointy. A wiry tail had sprouted from her lower back.

And, as Kitty leaped from countertop to breakfast table to the top of the kitchen cabinets, Juni could see that she had all the agility and strength of a tiger.

She was a cat-woman!

And clearly, she didn't want Carmen and Juni to know about her secret identity.

Which was a problem. Because Juni's allergies were just beginning to kick in. His nosed itched and his eyes watered. He suddenly realized that all day he'd been having an allergy attack because of Kitty!

Crouching by the kitchen door, he hid from the feline agent.

His chest began huffing and heaving.

His nose twitched.

He was going to sneeze!

Juni clapped his hands to his face, using one to squeeze his nose shut and the other to cover his mouth. Then he peeked over the island in the middle of the kitchen and tried to pinpoint Kitty's location.

She was batting a ball of string around the floor, meowing and purring happily. So far, she hadn't noticed Juni's intrusion.

Good thing she didn't morph into a blood-hound, Juni thought. As silently as he could, he crept out of the kitchen. Then he dashed down the hallway and up the stairs. He had to tell Carmen what he'd seen!

Juni hurried past the bathroom toward Carmen's room at the end of the hall. But then another sound made him stop in his tracks.

Splish, splash, splash.

Wincing, Juni turned around. The bathroom door was almost closed. The room was dark, but for the dim glow of a night-light.

And someone was in the bathtub.

Holding his breath, Juni squinted through the inch-wide space between the door and the door-jamb. All he could see through the gloomy light was an arm, lazily hanging over the bathtub's edge.

But when Juni's eyes adjusted to the dark, they began to bulge in disbelief.

That was no arm.

It was a sucker-covered tentacle!

Stifling a gasp, Juni dashed silently down the hall. He stole into Carmen's bedroom and ran over to her bed.

"Carmen," he whispered, shaking her shoulders violently. "Wake up! Major crisis."

Carmen's eyes fluttered open enough to glare at her brother.

"You have a bellyache from all that ice cream, don't you?" she said. "Guess what, Juni? That's no crisis. That's your own fault. But when I'm fully awake, you're really going to have a bellyache on your hands."

Juni clutched his stomach. Carmen was right—he was feeling queasier than ever. He wished that this was his only problem.

"Believe me," Juni said. "This is much, much worse. Wake *up*!" He shoved Carmen so hard, she tumbled right out of her bed. She stumbled to her feet and stared at her brother in outrage.

"Okay, bedhead," she said. "*Now* you're gonna pay."

She advanced on Juni, rolling up her pajama sleeves.

Before she could get any closer, Juni blurted, "Kitty's a cat, and Octavian's an octopus!"

It worked. Carmen stopped in her tracks.

"*What?*" she asked. Her voice was full of doubt.

"Well, not completely," Juni said. "Kitty's sort of a whiskery woman with really good pouncing skills. And Octavian's got tentacles. That's all I saw."

"Juni, do you know how insane you're sounding?" Carmen said. "Maybe all that butterscotch syrup went straight to your head."

"You've gotta believe me," Juni said. He slumped to the floor and leaned against the foot of Carmen's bed. Then he told her everything he'd just seen.

When he had finished, Carmen slumped to the floor next to him. She was stupefied.

"Our baby-sitters are beasts," she said.

"They're not just baby-sitters," Juni pointed out. "They're also spies."

"You're right," Carmen said. "We have to go to the OSS and get help."

"Let's get out of here," Juni said, leaping to his feet.

But Carmen stayed put. Her forehead was creased with worry and deep thought.

"Unless . . ." she said.

"Unless what?" Juni said. "Devlin's gotta hear about this, Carmen. There's not a minute to lose."

"Juni," Carmen said, getting to her feet and going pale. "Devlin specifically sent these new agents over here. Maybe . . . maybe he knew that Kitty and Octavian were mutants."

"But why would Devlin do that?" Juni said.

"Who knows?" Carmen said. "Maybe the OSS has gone evil! And they're using these animal agents to take us out."

"I can't believe that!" Juni said.

"Well, the other scenario," Carmen said, "is that our baby-sitters are double agents. They're out to take the OSS down—from the inside."

"The only way to find out for sure is to head to HQ," Juni said, clenching his fists. "We've got to get out of here. Now!"

"So soon?"

Carmen and Juni gasped and turned to the voice.

Kitty Lieder was poised in the doorway.

Her back was arched threateningly.

Her green eyes had squinted to evil slits.

Her long, red nails were flashing.

Kitty Lieder wasn't about to let Carmen and Juni go anywhere. Not without a catfight!

CHAPTER 5

Kitty was completely blocking the Spy Kids' exit.

"Stand back, Juni," Carmen said. "I'll handle this. C'mon in, Kitty Cat!"

Carmen uttered a growling "Hai!"

Kitty snarled a sinister "Meow!"

And then, the Spy Kid and the cat-woman leaped at each other.

Carmen lashed at Kitty with a roundhouse kick/jab combo. But Kitty dodged the assault easily. In fact, she leaped so high into the air to avoid Carmen's blows, her pointy ears grazed the ceiling. She swooped over Carmen's head and landed behind her. Then she grabbed Carmen in a hammerlock.

That's an easy one, Carmen thought. She pushed off the floor with her feet and did a back flip over Kitty's head. She wrenched herself free of the cat-woman's grip and landed near her desk.

That's when Carmen saw Juni foraging through her desk drawer.

Carmen's *private* desk drawer.

"Hey, Juni," she said, ducking a swipe of Kitty's claws and rolling across the floor. "Or should I call you Snoop dog? Just because we're in the middle of a battle doesn't mean you can paw through my stuff!"

"*Mrowr!*" Kitty squealed, jumping on Carmen and pinning her shoulders to the floor.

"Don't worry, I have no interest in your boring diary," Juni said. "I'm looking for something else."

Meanwhile Kitty sat on Carmen's stomach and leered into her face menacingly. Kitty's teeth had become sharp and pointy. She looked like she was ready to play with Carmen's nose like a Frisky Treat!

"*What* else?" Carmen grunted to Juni as she struggled within Kitty's grip.

But Juni didn't answer. In fact, Juni seemed to have disappeared! Carmen would have wondered where her brother had gone off to if Kitty hadn't chosen that moment to chomp down on Carmen's arm!

"*Aaaaiggh!*" Carmen screamed, before she realized that all Kitty had gotten was a mouthful of her flannel pajama top. Carmen heard a ripping noise. Kitty rolled away with a shred of Carmen's sleeve in her mouth and a venomous look in her eyes.

"Okay," Kitty said, spitting the fabric scrap onto the floor. "Enough of these cat-and-mouse games. You and your brother are in for a major beat—"

"Here, kitty, kitty, kitty," called a voice from across the room. Juni hopped off the bed and flashed a laser pointer at Kitty. It was the laser pointer that Carmen had used for her presentation on the Mayan ruins at school. *What is he going to do with that?* Carmen thought.

Pointing the laser toward Carmen's closet, Juni began edging toward Carmen's bedroom door. He shot his sister a pointed glance.

Carmen nodded back. A cat couldn't resist—and neither could Kitty. It was the perfect feline distraction.

Juni bobbed the laser along the wall as he and Carmen continued to inch toward the door. Finally, they'd made it!

Carmen grabbed the doorknob and flung the door open.

"Okay, Juni," she whispered. "Get ready to dash—*AAAAAHHHHHH!*"

Carmen leaped back from the door.

"What?" Juni cried, glancing through the door-way. "*AAAAAHHHH!*"

They were staring at Octavian Buss.

He was standing in the Spy Kids' way, leaning against the doorjamb with his elbows.

All eight of them.

Two of Octavian's arms had hands. The other six were lined with suckers.

What's more, the spy's shiny, bald head had turned slimy and gray. And his human mouth had been replaced by a snapping octopus's beak.

"Suckers *and* opposable thumbs," Carmen breathed. "Impressive."

"And let's not forget what Kitty's got," Juni whispered. "Night vision, agility and all the arrogance of a Persian cat."

"We could try to fight them," Carmen said skeptically.

"Or we could just go back to bed," Juni prompted. With a wink.

The octo-man and cat-woman began to advance menacingly on the Spy Kids.

"I'm thinking dreamland is looking pretty good right now," Carmen said.

"Oh, I don't think you'll be sleeping anytime soon, kittens," Kitty growled.

"Watch us," Carmen said. With that, she grabbed Juni's arm, and the two Spy Kids leaped onto her bed. Juni began to throw Carmen's pillows and blankets at the mutant invaders.

Meanwhile, Carmen lifted her reading lamp off her nightstand. In a cavity beneath the lamp was a tiny, numeric keypad. She quickly typed a combination into the pad. Then she glared at Kitty and Octavian.

"Nighty-night," she said, giving them a little wave.

Immediately, the bed's headboard tilted forward, revealing a large hole in the wall! Then the foot of the bed angled upward, tipping both Spy Kids into the hole.

As soon as Carmen and Juni slipped through the opening, the headboard snapped closed behind them—shutting Kitty and Octavian out.

Then the Spy Kids went for a ride. They tumbled and slid through a black, slick tunnel. In an instant, they'd landed—in the shrubs of their very own backyard.

"I *love* those escape hatches Mom and Dad installed last year," Carmen said, breathing heavily.

"Yeah," Juni said. "They're fail-proof!"

Suddenly, he heard a rattling noise in the tunnel.

"I think," he added, staring at Carmen.

As the rattling continued, the Spy Kids dove away from the tunnel and crouched behind a bush. Then they waited to see who would appear.

"That must be the sound of Kitty's claws, skittering down the escape hatch," Carmen whispered with a shiver.

"Or the sound of Octavian's arms," Juni whispered with a shudder.

Finally, their unknown foe tumbled out of the tunnel. It was . . . surprisingly small. And shiny.

And as soon as it hit the dirt, it bounced up cheerfully. Then it skittered on skinny, crablike legs straight to Juni and jumped into his lap.

"Ralph the Second!" Juni cried. He giggled happily as the robot scampered up his arm to perch on his shoulder. "You're the best personal robot ever!"

"Yeah, yeah," Carmen said, glancing up at the Cortez mansion. "I hate to break up the boy-bot lovefest, but we're not safe out here."

She pointed to the upstairs windows. The shadows of two figures were racing through the house. One had pointy ears. The other had way too many arms.

"They're looking for us," Carmen said.

"You're right," Juni said, giving Carmen a look. "Tree house?"

"Tree house," Carmen agreed through gritted teeth. "We wanted a mission of our own? Well, now we've got one."

The kids stole across the backyard and ducked behind a big, old, oak tree. They stood before the trunk. A burst of light popped out of it and scanned their faces.

"Your name?" said a robotic voice inside the tree.

"Carmen Elizabeth Juanita Echo Sky Brava Cortez," Carmen said firmly.

"Your name?" the tree asked Juni.

"Juni Rocket Racer Rebelde Cortez."

"Verified," the tree said. A small doorway in the trunk whooshed open. The Spy Kids stepped inside, and an elevator zoomed them up into the leafy treetop.

When they stepped inside their tree house, they finally allowed themselves a sigh of relief. When Uncle Machete had custom built the house for them, he'd installed an elaborate surveillance and security system. They'd be safe from Kitty and Octavian here.

They'd also be comfortable. Uncle Machete had also included in the tree house: a mainframe computer, a communications satellite, a full-size foosball table, a large-screen TV, and, most important, snacks!

"Ginger ale, at last," Juni cried. He ran to the minifridge and pulled out a bottle of soda. Taking a big swig, he walked back to Carmen. She'd flopped into a chair behind the computer terminal and grabbed the satellite phone. She logged into a secured line and began dialing a number.

"Mom and Dad's cell phone?" Juni asked, taking another gulp of ginger ale.

"Yup," Carmen said. She put the phone on SPEAKER and tucked her bare feet beneath her as the phone rang. "Let's see what they have to say about our 'baby-sitters.'"

Dad answered after the fourth ring.

"*Si?*" he said breathlessly. "Carmen, Juni?"

"It's me, Dad," Carmen said. "How are things in Rio? What's that noise?"

There were loud, clacking sounds echoing in the background. The kids also heard their mother's voice: "Hi-*yah*! Take that! And that!"

"Eh, Carmenita," Dad interrupted. "Our mission has taken an . . . unexpected turn."

"Are you all right?" Carmen asked in alarm.

"Oh, fine, fine," Dad said, huffing and puffing

as he did. "It's just, well, it seems these salsa dancers have turned into massive mutants. Half-crocodile, half-human. Your mother and I are fighting them off now."

"How *many* half-crocodiles?" Carmen shrieked.

"Oh, no more than twenty," Dad replied. "No problem. Eh, can you hold on a second, Carmen?"

"Sure," Carmen said.

She heard Dad's phone clatter to the ground. Then she heard several loud thwacking noises, a few more *hi-yahs*, and the scream of a wounded croc-man. After that, Dad got back on the line.

"Okay," he said, sounding a little more out of breath. "Where were we? Ah, yes, the crocodiles. Don't bother telling Juni. I don't want him to have nightmares."

Carmen winced as her father's voice echoed out of the speakerphone. Juni, of course, was listening to every word. He was staring at the phone, growing paler by the second.

"So," Dad continued, "how are things at home? Did Kitty make you dinner?"

"Listen, Dad," Carmen said urgently. "The OSS has set a trap. They're out to get us. Either that, or the agency's under atta—Dad? *Dad?!*"

She heard an echoey click. Then a dial tone.

Carmen stared at the phone for a moment. Then she looked up at her brother. He was clutching the ginger ale bottle in one hand, his aching stomach in the other. He looked a little green.

"The line's dead," Carmen said. "We're on our own."

CHAPTER 6

After sitting for a stunned moment in the eerily quiet tree house, Juni leaped out of his chair.

"We've gotta go to Rio!" he exclaimed. "Mom and Dad need our help."

He immediately went to the foosball table. Grasping a couple of the rods, which were lined with plastic men, he began to spin them. He whirled the blue guys to the left for two rotations, red guys left for three, then red guys right for six.

Because the foosball table wasn't just a foosball table, of course. It was also an elaborate combination lock.

As the last foosball guy spun into place, a whirring sound filled the room. The large-screen TV swung open, of course. Because it wasn't just a large-screen TV. It was also a safe, hiding the Spy Kids' emergency arsenal of spy bags, gadgets, parachutes, jet packs, freeze-dried cheeseburgers—the works.

Juni grabbed two of the spy bags and began tossing gizmos into them. Ralph the Second scampered into one of the bags as well. But Carmen remained frozen at the control panel, staring at the phone.

"While I'm packing," Juni said briskly. "You log onto the computer and find us a flight path to Brazil. While you're at it, find us something to fly *in*!"

"Maybe . . ." Carmen murmured.

Juni had just been dropping a handful of water-activated PB & J pellets into his spy bag. But Carmen's hesitation made him stop.

"'Maybe'?" Juni asked. "What's with the 'maybe'? Mom and Dad are in mucho trouble. And we're going to save them. That's what we do, Carmen."

"If mutant agents have infiltrated the ranks, the OSS is *also* in trouble," Carmen said. "Or if the entire OSS has been taken over by evil animal agents, who knows what kind of damage the agency could inflict on the citizens of this country, even the—?"

"World," Juni finished wearily. "I know this part. We have to save the world."

"It's what Mom and Dad would want us to do," Carmen said.

"But what if Mom and Dad can't handle those crocodiles?" Juni whispered. "What if they've been taken hostage or . . ."

Juni remembered the sound of the crocodiles' snapping jaws on the speakerphone. He thought of his father's breathless voice. His palms started sweating so much that several of the PB & J pellets in his hand erupted into full-fledged sandwiches.

". . . or worse," Juni said fearfully. He was so agitated, he didn't even take a bite of PB & J. He tossed the sandwiches onto the foosball table.

"Mom and Dad are two of the smartest spies in the world," Carmen said, getting to her feet. "We have to have faith in them. *And* we have to get to the OSS's HQ as soon as possible. We can't do a thing until we find out what the deal is with these mutants."

"All right," Juni said, looking down at his dirt-stained pajamas and bare feet. "Um . . . is today a dress-casual day at the OSS?"

"Not a problem," Carmen said, walking over to a closet next to the TV. She pulled it open to reveal a full spy wardrobe—black cargo pants, long-sleeved T-shirts, spy vests, and utility belts loaded with gadgets.

"Let's get changed and hit the road," she said.

A half hour later, the Spy Kids checked their surveillance system. There were still no signs of Kitty and Octavian, so they slunk from their tree house to the garage.

They skulked through the garage door and turned on the light. When they looked around the garage, they groaned.

"No!" Juni groaned. "Mom and Dad took our self-propelled electric car to the airport."

"And our jet scooters are in the shop," Carmen moaned.

"And HQ is too far away to reach with jet packs," Juni added darkly.

"Which leaves only . . . the Jumping Jack Flash!" Carmen wailed. "The car that brings new meaning to the word carsick."

"Even if it is, kinda cool-looking," Juni admitted.

He was right. The JJF was a perfect, cherry-red sphere, with a small, domed, flexiglass windshield and a large, arched handle on top. The handle hooked around the huge springloaded launching mechanism. It also made the JJF look a lot like a massive Hippity Hop ball.

"Hey, what are these?" Juni said, pointing to almost invisible nodules dotted around the JJF's surface.

"Oh, attachments of some kind," Carmen said. "I tried a few of them during the test drive. There were some suction cups, a mechanical arm, windshield wipers, stuff like that."

"Uncle Machete likes a car fully loaded, I'll give him that," Juni said, as he opened the JJF's hatch. "If he could just smooth out the ride, this would be the coolest vehicle ever."

"Tell me about it," Carmen complained. She and Juni climbed into the JJF and closed the hatch. They strapped themselves into the two seats. While Carmen flipped a few switches and turned over the JJF's ignition, Juni pressed the garage-door opener.

He watched the door slowly inch upward.

"You know what's funny?" Juni said, shoving his spy bag beneath his seat.

"Hmmm?" Carmen murmured. She was immersed in booting up the JJF's computer.

"We haven't seen a hint of Kitty and Octavian since we escaped into the tree house," Juni observed. "You don't think they just disappeared, do you?"

"Well, *we* did, didn't we?" Carmen said. "There's no way they could have known we were in the tree house. It's completely cloaked by high-tech security. So, maybe they figured they'd failed their mission and bailed."

"It all seems too easy," Juni said, suspiciously.

Carmen huffed in annoyance and turned to her brother.

"Juni, not *every* mission has to be fraught with danger, betrayal, and death-defying battles," she said. "Don't be such a pessimist. Sometimes things just work out."

"Yes, sometimes they do," said an oozy, burbly voice.

The kids froze. It was Octavian! He was taunting them through the JJF's exterior speakers. Which meant he was lurking just outside the Jumping Jack Flash!

Carmen and Juni looked at each other in silent alarm. Then Juni pointed frantically at the launch button. Carmen nodded and hit the button.

"*AAAAAAHHHHHHH!*" the kids screamed as the JJF shot out of the garage like a whirling, run-away pinball.

They hit the driveway with a bobbling skid and went sailing into the air. The JJF did a few lazy flips before it began its descent.

"Oh, man, we're gonna hit the neighbors' front lawn!" Carmen cried.

Crunch.

"Make that the neighbors' mailbox," Juni said, as the JJF bounced back into the air, this time arcing much higher. "But, hey, at least we ditched Octavian.

Then a sound came through the speakers.

The sound of a throat clearing.

And then, the oozy, burbly voice filled the JJF once again.

"Well, actually," the voice said, "now I think you're being a little too *optimistic,* Juni."

Trembling, the Spy Kids glanced up through their domed windshield.

Octavian Buss was leering down at them. His tentacles were fanned out all over the JJF's exterior. His suckers were holding him on tight. And clearly, he wasn't going to let go until he'd hitchhiked all the way to the OSS!

"Sometimes things just work out, huh?" Juni said to his sister. "Well, not this time. We've got a sticky situation on our hands."

CHAPTER 7

Carmen sprang into action. She began typing frantically on the JJF's computer terminal. A map of the vehicle's exterior sprang up on the screen.

Carmen scanned the JJF's gadget options. She quickly made a decision—and pushed a button.

Then she looked up through the domed windshield. Octavian Buss was still grinning down at the Spy Kids with a mad glint in his eyes. He didn't notice when two long, metal arms capped by robotic claws began rising up behind him. In the claw of one was a super soaking squirt gun. In the other—a windshield squeegee.

"Uh, Carmen," Juni said, eyeing the metal arms skeptically. "Is this any time to be worrying about bugs on the windshield?"

"Well, that's a pretty big bug!" Carmen said. She pushed a button labeled SQUIRT!

The squirt gun began pummeling Octavian with stinging jets of water.

"*Aaaaaahhh!*" the startled octo-man cried. He looked over his shoulder, just in time to see the windshield squeegee looming over him! The rubber blade began slicing and dicing at his slimy head. For a moment, Carmen thought the JJF might be overpowering the evil mutant, but Octavian's tentacles were stronger than Carmen had expected. While the villain used five tentacles to hang on to the Jumping Jack Flash, he swiped at the squeegee with a remaining suckery limb. He ripped the robotic arm completely off the hurtling JJF, tossed it into the air, and watched it plummet to the ground.

"Uh-oh," Carmen said. "This is bad."

What was worse, Octavian seemed to be enjoying the dousing of the supersquirt gun. As water dripped into his eyes, he grinned at Carmen.

"Thanks for the water," he said. "That was just the refresher I needed."

"Octopuses need water," Carmen said, slapping her hand to her forehead. "How could I forget?"

"Uh, Carmen," Juni said, looking queasy. "Did you forget we're also in a bouncing vehicle? And we're going dooooooowwwn!"

Indeed, the JJF was headed straight for a suburban street! Luckily, it was still the early hours of the morning and the road was deserted.

But, it was still pretty hard.

"Hey, let's flip it," Carmen suddenly proposed as the JJF catapulted toward the ground.

"Flip the JJF!?" Juni said. "I thought we wanted as little tumbling as possible. Remember the car sickness?"

Carmen glanced up. Octavian had already proved that he could hear every word that was said inside the JJF. So she leaned over to Juni's seat and whispered in his ear.

"Yeah, but if we hit the ground at just the right angle," Carmen said, "our stowaway just might go *splat*."

"Okay, let's flip it," Juni whispered back. "But how?"

"*Lean!*" Carmen ordered.

The Spy Kids tipped over in their seats.

But that wasn't enough to make the JJF wobble in the direction in which they needed it to go. They had to have more weight to unbalance the craft.

And Juni's spy bag was the heaviest thing they had. Or at least it would be—when Carmen added water to all the freeze-dried snacks inside.

She grabbed a bottle of mineral water from the mini fridge next to her feet and uncapped it. Then she reached beneath Juni's seat and grabbed his bag.

"Hey," he protested. "What are you—"

Carmen poured the water into the bag. A series of popping noises filled the JJF, and the bag began to sag in her hands. She could smell P B & J sandwiches and cheeseburgers and fries and cinnamon toast smashed up against popcorn.

"*Nooooo!*" Juni cried. "My snacks—they're ruined!"

"They're heavy!" Carmen corrected him. Then she tossed the spy bag to the far side of the JJF.

The craft began to wobble.

Then it veered. And tipped!

And finally, it turned over completely.

The Spy Kids looked up through the flexiglass windshield and watched. Octavian continued to cling to the JJF, oblivious to the pavement looming behind him.

Both kids began to yell as the JJF hit the ground.

Squiiiissh!

That was the sound of Octavian, being smooshed between the bouncing vehicle and the street.

Sproing!

And that was the sound of the JJF, resuming its wobbly, airborne arc.

Fearfully, the kids glanced up at the windshield.

They braced themselves for the sight of octopus innards—or something equally gross—smeared all over the glass.

Instead, they found themselves gaping at Octavian Buss—alive and well! And still grinning. Sure, his eyes looked a little more bulgy than usual. And a few of the teeth in his grotesque beak looked loose. But otherwise, the octo-man was just fine.

"Don't you kids know anything about octopuses?" Octavian cackled through the JJF's speakers. "I'm nothing but a big, smooshy mollusk. No bones! And no bones means no breaks! You can't beat me, kiddies."

"Wanna bet?" Carmen asked. Her hands clenched into fists and her eyes narrowed.

She unbuckled her seat belt and leaped out of her seat.

"Juni, take the wheel," she ordered.

"What are you doing?" Juni cried, moving over to Carmen's seat and grabbing the JJF's controls.

"Showing Mr. Mollusk that his suckers," Carmen said, "aren't so special."

She reached down and pressed a button on the toe of each of her spy boots. Suddenly, the rubber soles of the shoes erupted with dozens of tiny-but-powerful suction cups. Carmen strapped on a parachute, just in case. Then she climbed onto Juni's empty seat and popped open the JJF's hatch.

"Just keep us as steady as possible," Carmen said over her shoulder. "It's time for a little hand-to-sucker combat."

With that, Carmen did a reverse pull-up and shot up through the hatch. She landed on the exterior of the JJF and felt the suckers in her soles grab the surface. The wind whipped her long, dark curls into her face. Their altitude—hundreds of feet in the air—was terrifying.

But Carmen couldn't think about that.

Instead, she snuck up behind Octavian and grabbed one of the tentacles anchoring him to the JJF.

"What?" Octavian cried. He glanced behind him. When he saw Carmen yanking on one of his legs, he gave it an irritable twitch. The powerful limb sent Carmen flying.

Down inside the craft, Juni saw his sister go sailing through the air.

"No!" he cried. He was going to lose her!

In a panic, Juni hit all the JJF's gadget buttons at once. A stun-ray phaser shot out of one opening. Out of another—an automatic shovel. Suction-cup feet popped out of four nodules. And out of the last?

A giant net!

It caught Carmen an instant before she pulled her parachute's ripcord. Then it tossed her back toward the JJF. Her sucker shoes connected with a *pop*.

Then she reached into her spy vest.

"Time for the big guns, Octavian," she said.

She saw the octo-man's eyes widen in fear.

"You can't shoot me," Octavian said. "What if you damage this vehicle? With your *brother inside*? Ah-ha-ha!"

"Please, I'm twelve years old. I don't deal with firearms," Carmen said. "I am, however, a fabulous cook."

With that, Carmen pulled a bright red, succulent, three-pound lobster out of her pocket. Having a fully stocked tree house always came in handy!

Octavian gasped. Then he quickly recovered. He glanced away, trying to look indifferent. But Carmen could see him licking his beak with a long, slimy tongue.

Carmen waggled the lobster tauntingly at Octavian.

"Y'know," she commented. "Human beings and octopuses aren't so different, after all. We all *adore* juicy, rich lobster."

"Big deal," Octavian retorted. "I've got bigger shellfish to fry."

"Oh, yeah?" Carmen cried. The wind was whipping at her harder. The JJF was approaching the height of its arc through the air. Pretty soon, it would start plummeting back to earth! She only had seconds to get rid of Octavian and climb back inside.

"Let's see how resistible you really find it," Carmen said. "Catch!"

Carmen tossed the lobster into the air. Octavian gave an involuntary squeal and lunged at the food. Every one of his suckers unsucked from the JJF. Every limb reached for the shellfish.

And before he knew it, Octavian was floating in midair. He looked down at the ground. Then he looked up at Carmen.

And then he began to fall.

Carmen couldn't help but cringe as she watched the mutant plummet toward the ground. But suddenly, Octavian's fanned-out tentacles caught an updraft of air. His body took on the shape of a slimy umbrella. And instead of falling, he began to float, gently, toward the earth.

The lobster, of course, was not so lucky. It crashed to the ground, minutes before Octavian finally touched down himself.

Smiling with satisfaction, Carmen swung herself back inside the JJF. She took the wheel from Juni and said, "First thing we'll do when we talk to Devlin is get him to send some agents after our hungry octo-man."

"Not to mention, our feline foe—Kitty Lieder," Juni said. "But first, we have to *get* to the OSS."

"Not a problem," Carmen said, pointing through the windshield. Ahead of them was a giant, curlicue-shaped building. It was the OSS's HQ.

"We're just a couple more bounces away," Carmen said. "Fasten your seat belt. We're definitely gonna be making a crash landing."

CHAPTER 8

By the time Carmen and Juni reached the front door of HQ, the sun had risen. And the spies were battered and bewildered. After many clumsy bounces, they'd finally managed to land the JJF on the roof of the OSS. Then they'd used the fire escape to climb down to the building's front door. There was no way to get inside the heavily secured building without presenting their OSS ID badges to the guards.

"Maybe on the way home we'll take a taxi," Juni groaned as the kids slumped through the door. "I don't know which is worse. The JJF sickness or my hunger. I still can't believe you ruined all my freeze-dried food."

"Hello?" Carmen said. "Isn't our mission more important than your constantly complaining stomach?"

"I guess," Juni replied. He stepped up to the guard at the OSS door and flashed his badge.

"Agent Juni Cortez, requesting an audience with Mr. Devlin," he announced.

"Carmen Cortez, ditto," Carmen said, showing her own badge to the guard.

As the man dialed an internal phone, Juni looked at him. The guard had a head full of thick, white curls and a pale pink face. Juni had never seen him before.

"You're new here, aren't you . . . ?" Juni squinted at the guard's ID badge. "Officer Lamm? How do you like it at the OSS, so far?"

"Not ba-aa-aa-aa-aah-d," the guard said. Then he turned away from the Spy Kids and murmured into the phone.

Suddenly, Carmen grabbed her brother's arm, digging into his skin with her nails.

"Ow!" Juni said. "What's the problem?"

"Helloooo?" Carmen whispered, thunking lightly on Juni's head with her knuckles. "That guard just baaed like a sheep. And his name is Officer—"

"Lamm!" Juni gasped. "He's a woolly mutant."

"Which means the mutants have definitely infiltrated the OSS," Carmen said. "The question is, Does Devlin know yet? If not, we're gonna be the ones to tell him."

"But what if Lamm doesn't let us in?" Juni said.

"He has to," Carmen said. "How would it look if the OSS shut out their own Spy Kids? It would completely blow the double agents' cover."

Carmen glanced over Juni's shoulder and saw Officer Lamm hang up the phone. And just as expected, he nodded.

"Devlin will see you now," the mutant said. "His office is just up the corridor, down two flights of stairs, then around the . . ."

"We know the way," Carmen interrupted. "Thank you."

She grabbed Juni by the elbow, and the Spy Kids hurried through the security checkpoint. Then they began the long trek through the OSS's huge headquarters. Naturally, the office of Devlin, the OSS's head honcho, was in the building's most secure spot—dead center.

"Just keep your eyes and ears open," Carmen muttered. "Who *knows* how many of these mutants have infiltrated HQ."

The Spy Kids made their way through the twisty-turny hallways of the OSS. In the Research and Analysis wing, they walked through a maze of cubicles. An army of office workers was typing busily into computers. Juni glanced at a couple of the workers. Then he muttered to his sister, "Um,

Carmen? Is it just me, or do some of these typists look sort of strange?"

Carmen glanced at the clerks' pale, moist skin. Their long, fingers. Their bulging eyes.

"At first, I thought they just looked that way because they were computer geeks," Carmen murmured back. "But you're right. There's definitely an amphibious vibe in here. We'll have to tell Devlin about these guys, too."

The Spy Kids hurried through the cubicle complex and emerged in EGD—the Experimentation and Gadget Development wing. They tiptoed down a hallway lined with science labs.

Carmen and Juni peeked through the window of the first lab they came to. Inside, a crowd of scientists in white lab coats was standing around a large tank of water, making notes on clipboards.

And deep inside the tank, several slithery-looking OSS agents were swimming with agile grace, but they weren't wearing any oxygen tanks! And they never went up to the surface for air.

"Okay, those agents *could* be testing out a new water-survival gadget," Carmen said.

"*Or* they could be mutants," Juni said. "They do look pretty fishy."

The kids hurried on down the avenue of laboratories. Along the way, they passed another OSS worker pushing a cart of coffeepots and food trays. Carmen eyed the worker's thick mane of hair; her very long, flat nose; and her hooflike orthopedic shoes.

"A horse?" Carmen whispered to her brother.

"Of course," Juni replied, unleashing a small, sneeze. "Man, the place is crawling with animal agents. This is getting scary."

Finally, they arrived at Devlin's office. Carmen gave Juni a determined look, then rapped on the door.

"Come in!" Devlin called out.

Juni opened the door, and the Spy Kids marched inside.

"It's pitch-dark in here," Juni said.

"Um, Mr. Devlin?" Carmen called out.

The next thing the Spy Kids knew, four mechanical arms had reached out from the walls and grabbed them! The robotic arms shoved the kids into a couple of chairs and strapped them down with thick, canvas belts.

And then the chairs began to move! Actually, they began to zoom!

"What's happening?" Juni cried. He looked down at his feet. His chair was attached to a conveyer belt that was whizzing along at megaspeed. He glanced over his shoulder and saw Carmen's chair careening along behind his. The kids plunged into a dark tunnel. They veered through several passageways, whizzing so fast, they could barely breathe. They zoomed to the right. And to the left. Then they plunged down a steep, roller-coaster–like drop.

And finally, they approached a light at the end of the tunnel. When they reached it, the chairs screeched to a halt.

Breathlessly, Carmen and Juni glanced around. They were in a familiar office. One wall was covered with medals, diplomas, and glossy photos of world leaders. On the floor was shiny hardwood and an Oriental rug. In the center of the room was a mahogany desk and the back of a plush, leather chair. When the chair spun around, the kids found themselves staring at their boss.

"Mr. Devlin!" Carmen said. She looked awkwardly down at her tied-up self. "Um, that is new."

"Exactly," Devlin said, giving the kids a rakish grin. He jumped up from his desk and unfastened the Spy Kids' Velcro-fastened straps. They stood up, and the conveyer belt whisked backward out of the office. "It's my new security system. The director of the OSS can never be too careful."

Carmen and Juni nodded vigorously. Devlin motioned for them to sit in a couple of straight-backed chairs in front of his desk.

"Actually, that was a pretty cool ride," Juni said. He took a silver bag of chips out of his vest pocket and tore it open. He popped a few chips into his mouth. They tasted sort of puffy and sweet and strange. But Juni didn't care—he was starving! He crunched on a few more chips as he continued.

"And funny," he said, "that you should mention security, Mr. Devlin—"

"Yup!" Devlin said. "I tell ya, kids. You can't rest for a minute when you're a spy! You've gotta be ready for anything!"

"Um," Carmen said, "speaking of which—"

"For instance," Devlin went on, pacing excitedly in front of the kids' chairs. "We've got a new batch of agents that have just come out of the OSS training academy. They're brilliant, I tell you!"

"Oh?" Carmen and Juni said together. They gave each other sidelong glances.

"They're almost superhuman!" Devlin announced with an excited little snort. "I mean, if I didn't know better, I'd think some of these guys could climb walls without a rope. Or track an evildoer with their noses. Or see in the dark. But, of course, that's impossible. They're just highly skilled!"

Juni swallowed his mouthful of chips nervously.

"Actually, Mr. Devlin," Juni said, "that's a reality! We think the OSS has been infiltrated by mutants!"

"Yeah," Carmen piped up. "They seem to be half animal, half human."

"But they're all bad," Juni said. "Our baby-sitters attacked us!"

"What?" Devlin said. "That's ridiculous. Why would agents Lieder and Buss attack you?"

"Oh, I don't know," Carmen said with a diplomatic shrug. "Maybe they want to do away with all of the OSS's best agents and take over the agency for their own evil gain?"

Devlin glared down at Carmen.

"Just a hunch," she said with a nervous laugh.

"I think your head's still spinning from that little roller coaster ride, Carmen," Devlin said. "This 'mutant agent' idea is preposterous."

"But we've seen a lot of them," Juni cried. "A horse with a coffee cart. A sheep at the front desk. And some really slimy office workers."

"Are you contradicting me, Agent Cortez?" Devlin said. His crinkly brown eyes suddenly turned sinister. His teeth clenched in anger. He stopped pacing and placed his fists on his hips, staring down at Juni.

"No, sir," Juni squeaked. "Of course not. It's just that . . . we want to make sure you realize the OSS could be in trouble."

With that, Devlin's face softened. He nodded quietly. He grimaced thoughtfully.

"You know, you're right Juni," Devlin said. "The OSS *could* be in trouble."

Then, with lightning speed, Devlin whipped two ropes out of his suit pockets and whirled them around the Spy Kids. They were so shocked, they barely put up a fight.

In an instant, they were tied to their chairs—completely incapacitated by Devlin.

The leader of the OSS.

Their boss. The man they'd trusted completely, ever since they'd become spies.

"That's better," Devlin said. "*Now* the OSS is out of danger—with you meddling Spy Kids out of the way."

"Wh-what do you mean?" Carmen sputtered.

"Well, I've recently made a few changes around here," Devlin said. As he spoke, he reached beneath his arm and located a hidden zipper. With a tug, he opened the zipper all the way down to his ankle, then stepped out of his suit.

And his shoes. *And his skin!*

They hadn't been talking to Devlin at all! This was somebody else in an elaborate Devlin costume!

And that somebody was a plump, squat woman. Jiggly arms protruded from her tight OSS fatigues. Over her ample chest rested at least four chins.

And in the center of her fleshy face was a snuffly, soggy snout. The snout of a hog!

"From now on, we don't *save* the world, my Spy Kids," the woman declared in a piggy squeal. "We conquer it!"

CHAPTER 9

"**A***aaaaaaahhhh!*" Carmen and Juni shrieked.

If they'd thought Octavian was ugly and Kitty was creepy, then this woman was positively hideous. Pointy, pink pig's ears poked through her cap of matted blond hair. While her hands were those of ordinary humans, her feet were cloven pig's hooves.

"What have you done with Devlin?" Carmen cried. She struggled against the ropes that were binding her to her wooden chair. But she was trapped. So was Juni.

"Oh, don't worry about your boss," the pig-woman said in a voice that had gone shrill and squealy. "He's just a hop, skip, and a jump away."

"So, you've taken over the OSS," Juni growled. "You and your gross mutants."

"Gross!" the pig-woman bellowed. "How dare you! Do you know who you're talking to?"

"No, actually," Juni said with a shrug.

"I am Dr. Helga S.A. Hogg, the mastermind behind the OSS's new super spies," the woman announced. She puffed out her already puffy chest with pride. "For years I was a veterinarian at the national zoo. I would take care of crocodiles and jungle cats. In the aquarium, it was salamanders and octopuses. And, in the petting zoo, horses and sheep. And of course, lovely little pigs. But it drove me mad—positively *maaaad*—to see the waste."

"Waste?" Juni asked.

"Of their potential!" Dr. Hogg squealed. She pulled a cob of crunchy corn out of her desk drawer and began munching on it messily. "Potential for evil! With an animal's strength and a human's mind, there's nothing I cannot accomplish. Especially now that I've taken over the OSS! I'll turn this crime-preventing operation into a crime-committing one in no time."

"That'll never happen, Hogg!" Juni said. He struggled angrily against his bindings.

"Oh, but it already has," Dr. Hogg taunted. "I've got monkey-men burglarizing Tokyo. Cat-women crawling around New York City. And, as you know, my croc-men are doing a splendid job down in Rio."

Juni and Carmen gasped and glanced at each

other. Did that mean their parents had failed in their fight against the half-crocodiles?

They turned back to Dr. Hogg.

"How did you do this, Dr. Hogg?" Carmen demanded.

"Wouldn't you like to know!" Hogg replied. "I've developed a top-secret operation. One zap with my secret morphing ray and an OSS agent can become half cat, half octopus, or, best of all, half pig!"

"So, these mutants used to be human OSS agents?" Carmen said. "Hogg, you are truly despicable."

"You might want to tone down the insults, missy," Hogg said threateningly. She stuck her ugly snout into Carmen's face. "Unless you'd like to become half warthog!"

Carmen recoiled, but didn't lose her composure. She glared at Hogg defiantly.

"So, what'll it be?" Hogg said to them, waggling her piggy eyebrows.

"What do you mean?" Juni said.

"What would you two like to become?" Hogg said. "Half dog, perhaps, Carmen? Imagine the sleuthing power you'd have. And, Juni, I picture you as a half-frog. You could leap over skyscrapers in a single bound. Snare things with your long sticky tongue."

"Cooool," Juni breathed.

"Juni!" Carmen blurted.

"Oh, er, right," Juni said. Then he glared at Hogg defiantly. "Never, Dr. Hogg!"

"You dare to defy me?" the villain squealed.

"Uh-huh!" Carmen said, sticking out her chin.

"Have it your way," Hogg snorted. "I'll send some of my animal agents to transfer you to your cells."

"Cells?" Juni cried.

"Oh, yes, didn't I mention?" Dr. Hogg. "You're not the only OSS agents who've refused to be transformed. Those who have resisted are thrown into solitaire, in a place I like to call 'the barn.' A few weeks of eating out of troughs and submitting to my torture device—the milker—will change your minds, I guarantee."

With that, Hogg bustled plumply out of the office. She slammed the door behind her.

"The 'milker'?" Juni squeaked. "I don't even want to know what that is." Carmen didn't answer. She was too busy fidgeting.

"I have a laser cutter in my pocket," she grunted. "If I could . . . just get . . . to it. . . ."

Finally, she huffed in frustration and stared into her lap.

"I can't figure out any way to get through these

71

ropes," she said. "What do you think, Juni . . . Juni?"

Carmen looked over and saw—nothing! Juni had disappeared.

"Where'd you go?" Carmen screamed.

"Up here!"

Carmen looked up and saw Juni—and the chair he was tied to—floating in the air. He'd risen so high, his head was hitting the ceiling.

"Ow!" he winced.

"How'd you do that?" Carmen said. "And more important—why?"

"I don't know!" Juni said, panic in his voice. "One minute, I was down there. The next, I was floating into the air. My stomach feels all bubbly and puffed up."

Carmen gazed around the room in confusion. Her eyes fell on an empty silver bag on the floor. Juni had been munching chips from that bag when they'd first come into the office.

"Juniiii," Carmen said, squinting up at the bottom of her brother's shoes. His feet were fidgeting nervously. "Where'd you get that bag of chips you were eating?"

"I swiped it off that horse's coffee cart," Juni said. "I was really hungry!"

Carmen struggled against the rope that bound

her to her chair. She managed to extend her right foot enough to snag the silver bag with her toe. She flipped it over and squinted at the label.

"Just as I suspected," she said, her eyes widening. "That was no snack, Juni! That was a science experiment! They're weightlessness rice puffs—designed to help agents train for zero-gravity missions in outer space!"

"Well, they've given me another case of indigestion," Juni complained. He was still bobbing around beneath the ceiling. In fact, he was floating toward the office door.

"Your indigestion is the least of our problems!" Carmen snapped. "Couldn't you have read the label before you started stuffing your face?"

"You're just jealous because you can't float!" Juni taunted. He stuck his tongue out at his sister. "It's pretty cool up here!"

By then, Juni and his chair had floated clear across the room. His feet dangled in front of the door. The door—which was just beginning to open!

"Juni!" Carmen cried. "We've got company!"

"Shhh!" Juni whispered. "Let's give 'em a surprise!"

A hulking, slope-shouldered man with a red face, spiky horns, and a thick ring in his nose clomped into the office. He looked around the room for a moment. (Not thinking, of course, to look up.) Then he glared at Carmen.

"Where's the other Spy Kid?" the bull-man demanded. He pawed at the floor angrily with one hoof.

"Beats me," Carmen said with a snide shrug. As she gazed up at the animal agent, she saw Juni's spy boots float behind the bull's head.

"Oh!" Carmen said, innocently. "What's that behind you?"

The bull-man spun around.

"Wha—"

ZZZZZZZZ!

Instantly, Juni used the sole of one spy boot to jam a button on the other boot. His shoelace began whizzing out of his boot, extending until it had formed a long rope. Then, Juni began swooping his ankle in precise circles. Before the bull-man could react, Juni had lassoed him! The mutant's arms were pinned to his sides, and his legs were tied together. Juni gave his foot a swift jerk. The mutant crashed to the floor, thunking his head on the desk as he went. He was knocked out cold!

"Ha!" Juni yelled. He pushed another button on his boot, which detached the super long lace.

"Those bullfighting lessons Dad gave me really came in handy."

Then Juni gave Carmen a funny look.

"My stomach is feeling strange again," he said as he bobbed against the ceiling. "It feels like all the bubbles inside of me are . . . popping!"

He opened his mouth and unleashed a loud belch.

"Ew!" Carmen said.

"Excuse me-*AAAAAAH*!" Juni cried. The burp had apparently expelled all the floaty gas from his gut. He was plummeting to the floor!

Juni hit the hardwood with a loud crash. The impact smashed his chair to smithereens. Juni lay still for a moment.

Carmen screamed. "Are you okay, Juni?"

Slowly, Juni nodded. Then he stood up, shaking off his ropes and splintered chair bits. A few seconds more and his bleariness had disappeared. He was ready for action.

His first action, of course, was to run to Carmen's chair and untie her.

"Looks like those weightlessness puffs are quick-digesting," he said as he loosened the last knot in her ropes. "Lucky for us. *And* my stomach. Now, let's get out of here!"

CHAPTER 10

The Spy Kids poked their heads out of Helga Hogg's subterranean office. They gazed up at the steep tunnel that had brought them there. All they could see was blackness.

"The question is, *How* do we get out of here?" Carmen whispered.

Juni stepped gingerly out into the tunnel.

"Remember what Dr. Hogg said when we first arrived?" he said. "'The director of the OSS can never be too careful.' She's paranoid. Which means, there's got to be some hidden escape route."

He felt along the walls, looking for a switch, a secret doorway—something. But he couldn't feel a thing.

That's when Carmen noticed the floor of the tunnel. It was made of dirt! Moist, dank dirt at that.

"Huh?" Carmen said, putting a finger to her temple. "Why would Hogg have put soil outside her office . . ."

And suddenly, Carmen knew just what to do. She dropped to the floor and started pawing at the dirt.

"What are you doing?" Juni said, gaping at his sister.

"Looking for something," Carmen murmured.

"Looking for what?" Juni asked. "Buried treasure?"

"Yeah, actually," Carmen muttered. Then she felt something soft and knobby. It was half-buried in the soil. She scraped away a bit more of the dirt and grabbed the object, pulling it out of the ground.

Immediately, a doorway slid open on the far side of the tunnel. Juni ran over and peeked inside.

"It's an elevator!" he cried. "Come on!"

The Spy Kids jumped into the elevator, and the doors slid shut. Carmen was still clutching the dusty, knobby thing in her hand.

"What is that, a mushroom?" Juni asked.

"A truffle!" Carmen said triumphantly. "It's sort of like a mushroom, but much better and very expensive. In France, they use pigs to sniff out truffles in the woods. Pigs *adore* them. I read about it in my animal book."

"So, every time she wants to use this secret elevator," Juni said, "Helga *also* gets a snack to go. I can understand that."

"Of course, you can," Carmen said, rolling her eyes. "Okay, here's a button for the rooftop helipad! It'll take us straight to the JJF. Let's move!"

A few minutes later, the Spy Kids were safely away from the OSS. Safely, of course, being a relative term. Because they were again bouncing along in the Jumping Jack Flash.

"Okay, we need to make a plan of action," Carmen said. She was staring intently through the JJF's windshield and trying to steer the bouncing ball into unpopulated areas. "The OSS has been taken over by mutants. I think that's more than a two–Spy Kid job."

"Yeah, we definitely need reinforcements," Juni said. "As in, Mom and Dad."

"We've *got* to reach them!" Carmen said. "I'm going to try hacking my way onto their line of communication. You drive."

"Oh, already I don't like the division of labor here," Juni groaned as he grabbed the wheel. The JJF immediately began wobbling and veering.

"Keep it steady!" Carmen said, as she flipped open her laptop. She began typing frantically. Her satellite modem hummed.

"Okay, Mom's laptop isn't responding," Carmen said. "Let's try Dad's cell phone."

"Flock of birds!" Juni cried, jerking the wheel to the right.

"Aaaah!" Carmen cried, grabbing her laptop before it crashed to the floor. "Juni, watch where you're going!"

"I am!" Juni said. He was glaring through the windshield and sweating. "I *saw* the flock of birds, didn't I? And now I see—a small plane!"

This time, Juni jerked the wheel to the left.

Carmen flopped sideways in her chair. She threw out her left hand, barely stopping herself before her forehead hit the JJF's control panel. Her noggin was safe, but the impact made her OSS bracelet fly off her wrist! It crashed to the floor, and the moonstone charm split in two.

"Oh, no!" Carmen cried. "Mom just gave me that bracelet! Juni, your driving stinks."

"Sorry!" Juni said with a scowl.

Carmen leaned over as far as her seat belt would allow and grabbed her fractured bracelet from the floor.

"Bummer," she muttered, staring at the split moonstone. When she turned the charm over, though, she gasped. A red light was flashing from inside the charm. Flipping the charm back over, Carmen popped the moonstone shards out of their silver setting. Then she found herself staring at a tiny, activated mini-computer disk!

"This wasn't just an OSS charm bracelet," Carmen blurted out. "There's data in here!"

Carmen grabbed the mini-disk and pulled an inflatable floppy disk from her laptop case.

"Good thing the OSS sent me their latest software *before* the evil Hogg took over," Carmen said. She blew the disk up to full-size, popped in the mini-disk and inserted the whole thing into her computer.

Suddenly, Mom's face filled the screen.

"Hey!" Juni said, glancing away from the windshield. "What's Mom doing there?"

"Keep your eyes on the road," Carmen said, looking up from her laptop. Through the windshield, she saw clouds. "I mean sky . . . I mean *road*."

Because the JJF was indeed plunging downward again. Juni steered the vehicle onto a dirt road, and they bounced back into the sky.

"Hi, Carmen," Mom's video image was saying. "Remember what I said about mother-daughter spies sticking together? Well, this secret software will help us do just that. This disk contains highly sophisticated tracking technology. Your father and I are wearing homing devices in our own OSS bracelets. If you ever need to find us, you can hunt us down with this software."

"Perfect!" Juni said, barely missing a treetop with the JJF.

"So, I guess if you're implementing this disk, it means I'll be seeing you soon," Mom was saying with a smile. "Be careful, sweetie. And remember to be nice to Juni."

"Yeah!" Juni said, sticking his tongue out at Carmen.

"Whatever," Carmen said. Then she gasped as a map of South America popped onto the screen. Two flashing letters—an M for Mom and a D for Dad—were moving across the map. And they were nowhere near Rio! In fact, they were heading toward Carmen and Juni's location.

"Yes! Mom and Dad have escaped the crocodiles!" Juni said. "We can rendezvous with them when they get back and rescue the OSS together."

"Either that," Carmen said, "or the mutants have captured them! Which means we have to save them and *then* rescue the OSS together."

"Oh," Juni said, hanging his head. "I hadn't thought of that."

"It happened to us," Carmen reminded him grimly. "Either way, we've got to find them.

According to this software, they're traveling at maximum velocity."

"The question is," Juni said with a tremble in his voice, "where exactly will they end up?"

"Wherever they do, we'll be there!" Carmen said. "So, just keep this contraption bouncing, Juni. Our parents' lives may depend on it!"

CHAPTER 11

A half hour later, the M and the D on Carmen's computer screen came to a rest. The Spy Kids quickly tracked down their location. Then they made another crash landing. This time in a debris-littered field. Quickly, they scampered out of the JJF and crawled to a hiding place in some tall weeds.

"Where are we?" Carmen wondered. She glanced at her spy watch. She'd connected it to her laptop with a wireless modem. That way, she could keep an eye on her parents' locations while she and Juni were on the move. Mom and Dad seemed to be staying put at a location about a thousand feet northeast.

Juni grabbed his zoomable periscope from his gadget belt and extended it above the weeds in which the kids were hiding. Then he took a quick look around.

When he pulled the periscope away from his eyes, he looked pale.

"What was that place that Dr. Hogg told us about?" Juni said. "Where you eat out of troughs and face 'the milker'?"

"The barn?" Carmen said.

"That's what I was afraid of," Juni sighed. "Take a look."

Carmen squinted through the periscope and gasped.

"Juni," she breathed, "please, tell me you've got the 'zoom' on with this periscope."

"I wish," he said.

Carmen was looking at a barn, complete with red siding, white doors, and a silo on one corner. The only difference was the barn's enormous size. It was as wide as a city block and at least three stories tall!

"This must be where Dr. Hogg creates her mutants!" Carmen said. "Mom and Dad could have already been turned into half-crocodiles."

"Or cat-people!" Juni said. "I'd be allergic to my own parents!"

"We've got to get in there," Carmen said, biting her lip. She pressed the periscope to her eye again and hit the zoom button. She honed in on every door and window in the barn.

"Every entrance is heavily guarded," she said to

Juni. "Looks like mostly half-crocodiles and more gross octo-men."

"So," Juni said, popping the suckers out of the soles of his spy boots. "We start at the top."

Then he pointed slyly at the roof.

"Not bad," Carmen said with a grin. She pushed a button on her spy vest. A cable with a powerful grabber shot out of the vest and into her hand. Juni nodded and deployed his own grabber. The Spy Kids crept toward the barn. When they'd reached the building's base, they shot their grabbers up to the roof.

They yanked on the cables to make sure they were secure. Then they planted their suckery spy boots on the barn wall and began to climb. In just a few minutes, they'd reached the roof.

"Okay," Carmen said, walking up to a skylight. Pulling out a tiny auto-drill, she loosened several screws and removed the domed glass. The kids stole inside the barn. They walked carefully along the ceiling with their popping sucker shoes. Then they hung upside down for a moment, surveying the scene.

It was breathtaking—breathtakingly evil.

Like a warehouse or airport hangar, the barn was a cavernous, open space. Partitions divided it up into many, maze-like corridors. Occasionally, these narrow pathways culminated in tarp-covered rooms.

The Spy Kids couldn't see what was happening in the rooms.

But they could hear it. They heard loud zaps, followed by bestial barks and squeals. They heard moans of pain and shrieks of protest. And they heard a loud, sloshy noise that could only have been "the milker."

Gritting her teeth, Carmen whispered, "Time to hit the floor and start searching."

Latching their grabbers onto a heavy, wooden beam, the kids popped their sucker shoes off the ceiling. Then they pressed more buttons in their spy vests, extending their grabber cables. They whizzed down to the floor so fast, they blurred.

But apparently, they hadn't moved fast enough.

Just as they dropped into one of the corridors, two pig-men came down the hall.

"Intruders," they oinked. "Intruders!"

"Hey, Wilbur!" Carmen called. She reached into her vest pocket and pulled out something small and round and dusty.

The pig-men skidded to a halt. They sniffed the air with deep, snuffling snorts.

"Truffle!" they oinked.

"Go fish," Carmen said. She tossed the truffle high into the air. It flew over the corridor's partition. The pig-men glanced at the Spy Kids, then at one another. And then they went galloping down the hallway, snorfling at the ground, desperate to beat one another to the single, small truffle.

"That's one magical mushroom!" Juni marveled. "Okay, so what's your read on Mom and Dad?"

Carmen crouched on the barn floor and clicked a few buttons on her spy watch. Then she looked up and squinted down the corridor.

"This way!" she whispered.

Staying low to the floor, the Spy Kids crept through Helga Hogg's evil labyrinth. Every time they came to a fork in the corridor, Carmen consulted her spy watch. And then they crept onward.

Finally, the kids were almost upon the little M and D on Carmen's electronic map. As they approached the final turn in the corridor, Carmen began to run.

It feels like so long ago that I was watching Mom pack up her spy bag, she thought, biting her lip.

It was only now that Carmen admitted to herself how badly she wanted to find her parents. And how worried she was for them.

She veered around the corner and skidded to a stop. Juni wheeled around the corner, too, crashing into his sister with a grunt.

They looked around wildly. They were still stuck in Dr. Hogg's maze. There was no torture chamber, no laboratory, and definitely no Gregorio and Ingrid Cortez.

"Where are they?" Juni demanded. He grabbed Carmen's wrist and scrutinized the map on her spy watch.

"You must have read it wrong," he accused.

"I didn't!" Carmen insisted. "This is some sort of trick."

"Hey, what's that?" Juni said suddenly. He was pointing at something glinty on the floor.

Carmen rushed over and fell to her knees. Then she picked up two silver link bracelets. One had a moonstone charm, and the other, a chunky, turquoise one. She would have recognized them anywhere: Mom and Dad's OSS bracelets.

Juni took the turquoise bracelet out of Carmen's hand and gazed at it sadly.

"I wonder what these little hairs are," Juni said. He picked a tuft of wiry brown and black hair off the bracelet. When Carmen took a closer look at Mom's bracelet, she found black and white hairs on it.

"Aaaah-*choo*!" Juni sneezed.

"Shhhh!" Carmen said, glaring at Juni. "You want to get us caught? Clearly, Mom and Dad are being held by some furry mutants. We've got to find them, quick!"

"Where should we start looking?" Juni asked, handing Dad's bracelet back to Carmen. "Aaahh-*choo*!"

Just after Juni tried—and failed—to stifle his noisy sneeze, Carmen heard a sound.

Feeling herself go pale, she turned toward the noise.

Clack-grrrrrr-CLACK!

Sure enough, two figures appeared from around the corner. They had the brawny, brooding bodies of men, and long, snapping, menacing crocodiles' jaws—jaws that were gnashing and snapping at the Spy Kids!

"Well, that makes our decision easier," Carmen said, slowly backing away from the ghastly, green guards. "We'll just go in whatever direction these mutants chase us. *Run!*"

CHAPTER 12

Carmen and Juni wheeled around the corner and began sprinting through Helga Hogg's maze.

"What does your animal book say about crocodiles?" Juni said, huffing, as he ran a step or two behind his sister.

"They eat *everything*," Carmen shrieked. "Faster, Juni! They're catching up with us."

"*Everything*, you say?"

Suddenly, Juni stopped running. Waggling his eyebrows, he unhooked a lime-green, ray-gun-shaped gadget from his utility belt.

Carmen skidded to a halt, too.

"Are you crazy?" she demanded. "Keep running!"

Juni shook his head and pressed a few buttons on the ray gun.

"I've been dying to use this gizmo!" he said breathlessly.

"Interesting choice of words, Juni," Carmen cried.

The croc-men were lumbering ever closer.

Their jaws were snapping louder and louder.

Their beady, reptilian eyes narrowed to threatening slits.

Then Juni pulled the trigger on his ray gun. An acid-yellow Holo-Goon leaped out of the gizmo. This one was tall and angular. Tufts of cherry-red hair sprang out of its oversized ears. It had only three toes on each foot.

"Bleagh," the cartoon monster taunted the croc-men.

He stuck out his tongue at the mutants. Then he began to do a little dance.

The mutants' eyes swung from the Spy Kids to the Holo-Goon. For a moment, they seemed torn. Who should they attack first?

The Holo-Goon was closer.

So the croc-men pounced on it! They snapped at the three-dimensional cartoon monster with all the force in their long, toothy snouts. When their jaws closed upon nothing but air, they got confused.

Then they got mad.

And then the simpleminded mutants started snapping at the Holo-Goon even harder.

Meanwhile, Carmen and Juni sprinted away, weaving their way deeper into a maze of corridors.

"By the time those beasts realize he's just a Holo-Goon," Juni huffed as he ran, "we'll be long gone."

"Thanks!" Carmen puffed.

"Thank Kitty and Octavian!" Juni laughed. "They wanted a distraction? They got one. *Aaahh-choo!*"

Carmen stopped at an intersection in the maze.

"Hey," she said. "That's the first time you've sneezed since we found Mom and Dad's bracelets."

"Well, I can't help it!" Juni said, wiping his nose with his sleeve.

"No, it's a good thing!" Carmen said. "We can follow your nose to them! Keep going, Juni. The worse you feel, the closer we are."

"Great," Juni groaned. "*Ah-chooo!*"

Then he pointed to his right.

"This way," he announced.

They wended their way through the endless corridors. When Juni stopped sniffling, they changed directions. And whenever he sneezed, they pressed onward.

Finally, they turned yet another corner. But this time—they found themselves in one of the mysterious rooms.

The hairy mutant guards Carmen and Juni had

expected were nowhere to be seen, so they were able to survey the room. It was bare and foreboding—furnished with nothing but two tall gurneys. These cots were crisscrossed with leather straps. Metal skullcaps and electrodes strung with curly wires rested at the gurneys' ends. The wires were attached to a humming computer. Next to the computer was a tray filled with Gothic-looking medical instruments, as well as cotton balls, rubbing alcohol, and silicon gel—which both kids knew was a conductor for the electrodes.

The room was very creepy.

And perfectly silent.

Until Juni launched into a tremendous sneezing fit!

"No!" Carmen urged him. "We're gonna get caught."

"I can't—*ah-choo!*—help—*snorfle*—it!" Juni said.

Then Carmen heard another sound. A whimper from the far end of the grisly procedure room. For the first time, Carmen noticed something against the wall—two cages covered with heavy, opaque cloths. The whimpering sound was coming from them.

Carmen tiptoed over to the cages, terrified of what horrible mutants she might find underneath the tarps.

But knowledge is power, she told herself. She needed to know what was under those covers. Which meant, she needed to suppress her fears.

She glanced at Juni, who was still sneezing and snuffling wildly. Then Carmen turned back to the cages and gritted her teeth with determination. Bracing herself for something gross and scary, she ripped the covers away with one swift motion.

Then Carmen's eyes bugged out.

Her mouth dropped open.

And a single word escaped her stunned lips: "Aaaaw!"

She was staring at two of the cutest dogs she'd ever seen!

"Look, Juni!" she cried, as one of the dogs licked her hand through the cage's wires. "They're not mutants at all. Aren't they adorable?"

"Yeah," Juni admitted, "in a sneezy kind of way. *Ah-choo!*"

Carmen gave the dogs a hard look.

"I recognize these breeds from my book," she said. She pointed at the pretty black-and-white dog with the green eyes. "This one's a Norwegian elkhound."

Then she reached into the cage and scratched

the ears of the big, square-jawed brown dog. "And this guy here is a Spanish mastiff. Aren't you, boy?"

The male dog barked in agreement.

Or maybe it was alarm.

In fact, it wouldn't stop barking until Carmen looked over her shoulder. When she did, she saw two, slimy, sinister octo-men looming behind Juni. Juni was sneezing so hard, he didn't hear them coming.

"Juni!" Carmen cried. "Behind you!"

Juni spun around and sneezed again—spraying spit and snot right into the eyes of the menacing mutants.

"Good shot!" Carmen cried.

"Oh . . . uh, yeah, I meant to do that," Juni fudged. Then he dropped into a fighting crouch and prepared to do battle.

Sixteen arms and two beaks, Juni thought to himself. Uh, I can handle that. I . . . hope. "I got this," he called to Carmen.

The octo-men took a few squishy steps forward.

Juni backed up a few steps.

The octo-men advanced some more.

And, desperately, Juni backed up some more.

Crash!

"Whoa!" Juni cried. He spun around just in time

to see the medical cart that he'd backed into go crashing to the floor. When it landed, the tray of supplies went flying into the air.

The bottle of alcohol hit Juni on the shoulder.

The cotton balls rained down upon his head.

And the silicon gel bottle popped open and spurted cold, slippery goop all over Juni's head and torso.

"Ew!" Juni cried, looking down at his beslimed self. Then he looked up and screamed again.

Tentacles. All he saw was tentacles. While he'd been distracted, the octo-men had grabbed him and wrapped him tight in their suckery arms! And now they were lunging at him with their snapping, razor-sharp beaks. They were squeezing Juni so tight, he could barely breathe!

"Carmen," he tried to rasp. "Help!"

But Carmen's back was to him. She didn't hear a word.

Carmen was staring into the warm, green eyes of the Norwegian elkhound.

"There's something about this dog that's so . . . familiar," she said to herself.

Suddenly, Carmen froze.

She gazed into the elkhound's sad, sweet eyes.

She glanced at the mastiff's strong, square chin. And then she gasped.

"Mom! Dad!" she cried. "It's you!"

The dogs barked joyfully.

"Don't worry," Carmen announced as she jumped to her feet. "I'll fix this. Somehow . . ."

Suddenly, the mastiff, er, Dad, stared over Carmen's shoulder and began barking madly. Carmen spun around to see her brother, smashed within the suckery grips of the octo-men! They were snapping at Juni's head with their beaks. So far, all they'd gotten were mouthfuls of Juni's unruly, red curls.

"Juni!" Carmen screamed. She dashed over and grabbed Juni's shoulders, giving them a tremendous yank. To the Spy Kids' surprise, Juni slipped right out of the octo-man's grip! He and Carmen landed on the floor in a heap.

"How did that happen?" Carmen said. Then she took a closer look at Juni, who was all slimy and goopy. "Ew! Did that octopus slobber all over you?"

"It's that silicon gel," Juni said, "It must have made me too slippery to hang on to."

"For once, your clutziness comes in handy!" Carmen said. Before Juni could zing back a retort,

Carmen held up her hand. "Listen, I've got to deal with the dogs. Aka Mom and Dad."

"No!" Juni cried.

"Yes!" Carmen insisted.

Juni's heart sank. Then it was true. His parents had become furry animals. Furry animals to which he was violently allergic. Maybe he really *would* have to move into the backyard now!

Carmen's urgent voice shook Juni out of his pity party.

"Do you think you could hold off the octo-men for a few minutes?" she asked.

Juni grabbed the half-empty container of silicon gel off the floor.

"With this stuff, I can," he said. He began squirting the gel all over his arms and legs.

"There's a more important question," Juni said to his sister. "Can you save Mom and Dad?

CHAPTER 13

Carmen ran back to the dogs' cages and dug through her spy vest pockets for her acid crayon. As she searched, she saw one of the octo-men grab Juni. Her brother slid out of the villain's grip like a huge piece of Jell-O.

"Get a grip, mutant," Juni taunted. He leapt to the other side of the procedure room and waggled his fingers at the enraged octo-men. Then he glanced over his shoulder at Carmen. "Get it? Get a *grip*?"

Carmen merely rolled her eyes, but the two dogs barked appreciatively.

"Okay, if I had any doubts about who you are, that squashes them," Carmen muttered to the dogs. "*Only* Mom and Dad would laugh at one of Juni's corny jokes."

Finally, she found her acid crayon and skimmed it across the bars of the cages. They melted away with a sizzling sound until there were two gaping holes in the cages. The dogs leaped out and hopped up onto the gurneys.

"I know, I know," Carmen said to them. "I have to change you back into humans. The question is, How?"

"By hacking," Juni called out, as the octo-men grabbed him once again. He slipped out of the mutants' tentacles with a squelching noise. "C'mon, Carmen. This is your area."

"You're right," Carmen said, squinting at the clunky computer.

She grabbed the almost empty bottle of silicon gel off the floor and dabbed some of the stuff onto the dogs' furry heads. Then she attached the wired skullcaps to them.

She took a deep breath and gazed at her feet.

Okay, she thought, there are three possible scenarios here. I could figure out how to change these dogs back into my parents. Or I could turn them into horrible mutants. Or . . . I might fry their brains!

By the time Carmen got to scenario number three, she was trembling. But then she felt a warm, scratchy paw touch her hand. She looked up in surprise and saw the elkhound, her mom, looking deep into her eyes. And—Carmen knew dogs couldn't smile—but she could have sworn her mother had. Then she uttered one soothing bark.

You can do it, Carmen knew her mom was saying. And that's what gave Carmen the strength to square her shoulders, march to the computer, and start hacking.

She quickly became immersed in Dr. Hogg's encrypted data. She deciphered it within seconds. Then she began burrowing deep into the evil pig-woman's mutation formulas. In a few moments, Carmen thought she had come up with a reversal formula. She just hoped she was right!

As she typed in her formula, she dimly heard Juni's surprised voice behind her: "Hey, I guess the octo-men got fed up! They up and left. Whoo-hoo!"

But the comment barely registered with her. She was deep in hack-mode now. And she'd almost cracked the code.

A few keystrokes later, she was done.

She looked up at Juni and nodded.

Then she looked at the dogs strapped to the gurneys and flashed a tremulous smile.

Then she turned back to the computer and hit ENTER.

A tremendous blue spark surged through the air. The lights throughout the barn crackled and dimmed for a moment. Then a poof of smoke sur-rounded the dogs, who each gave a yelp of terror.

"Mom, Dad!" Juni cried. "Are you there?"

There was a long, long pause.

Carmen's stomach lurched.

Juni felt his hands break out in a cold sweat.

But then, a deep, Spanish-accented voice emerged from the smoke cloud.

"We're here, Junito," the voice said. "Good job with those octopus men, son!"

"You're back!" Carmen squealed. She and Juni plunged into the smoke, waving their hands and coughing. When the haze dissipated, there were Mom and Dad—still wired to the computers, but fully human.

The Spy Kids unhooked their parents from the metal skullcaps. Dad jumped off the table and looked at Mom. She was wearing her red tango dress, and Dad was wearing his dancing tuxedo.

"We were still disguised as ballroom dance con-testants when the crocodiles overpowered us," Mom explained. She hopped off her gurney with a little shimmy of her fringe.

"Yes, we look pretty snazzy, eh, kids?" Dad said, opening his arms wide. "Good as new."

He spun in a circle, showing off his shiny suit,

his cool red cummerbund, and his fluffy, perfectly groomed tail.

His . . . tail?

Carmen shrieked. Juni stifled a belly laugh. And Mom bit her lip.

"Uh, Gregorio?" she said. "I hate to be the one to tell you, but . . ."

"What?" Dad said innocently.

"It's . . . um," Mom said awkwardly, "it's just that . . . you seem to still have a tai—"

Grrrroowwrrr!

"Uh-oh," Juni said. He whirled around to face the sound, which was coming from the door to the procedure room. "I guess those octo-men weren't retreating after all."

"Nope," Carmen agreed grimly, "they were going for reinforcements."

A *lot* of reinforcements. In fact, there were so many mutants crowding into the room—half-pigs, half-octopuses, half-crocodiles, and even a half-tiger—that there was barely room for the Cortezes.

The tiger-woman seemed happy to solve the problem—by seeking to devour them. She paced back and forth in front of the cornered Cortezes, licking her whiskery chops and purring loudly. She began to stalk toward Juni.

"Grabber!" Carmen yelled to her brother.

"*I* don't want to grab her," Juni cried. "*You* grab her!"

"No!" Carmen shouted, rolling her eyes. "Your grabber cable. Use it!"

"Oh!" Juni said. "Well, ya don't have to tell *me* twice."

Juni, along with the rest of his family, leaned backward and pushed the button on his vest that unleashed his grabber and cable. All of their claws whizzed upward and latched onto a ceiling beam. Then, they all pushed their retract buttons.

"Later, alligator!" Juni yelled as the family whizzed upward.

When they reached the ceiling, they hovered for a moment to make a game plan.

"We've got to get to Dr. Hogg!" Carmen explained to their parents. "She's a veterinarian-gone-bad. She's the mastermind behind these mutants. And she's trying to take over the OSS!"

"*And* she's done something with Devlin!" Juni piped up. "That wasn't him who sent you to Rio. That was Helga S.A. Hogg in disguise!"

"What?" Mom said. "I bet that's why we had to sit in the last row of economy class on our flight!"

"There was no movie and the in-flight meal was

terrible!" Dad sputtered. Then he glanced over his shoulder.

"Plus—I seem to have a tail!" Dad added as his fluffy new appendage fluttered out behind him. "Where is this . . . Hogg?"

"Well, that's the problem," Carmen said. "We haven't seen her since we escaped from Devlin's office, where she was holding us hostage."

When Carmen uttered those words, Dad's face went dark.

"This villain held *my* children hostage?" he raged.

Suddenly, Dad pushed his CABLE-EXTEND button and whizzed down to the floor.

"Dad, what are you doing?" Carmen yelled.

"Be right back," Dad called up to them.

And he was, too. But this time, he was clutching a pig-man by the mutant's curly tail.

"That hurts!" the mutant oinked.

"Tell me about it," Dad bellowed, flicking his own tail angrily. "Now tell us, where is this Helga Hogg?"

"Never," the evil minion answered.

"Listen, little pig," Mom said, swinging over on her cable until she was dangling nose-to-snout with the mutant. "If you don't squeal, my husband might lose his grip. And then your friends down there are going to be having your ribs for dinner."

"Even your spare ones," Juni added with a glare.

"I saw the way that half-tiger was looking at you," Carmen taunted. "Like she was dreaming about pork chops."

"All right," the trembling pig cried. "Dr. Hogg is at the OSS, in the situation room. But you're too late. By the time you arrive at HQ, our leader's takeover will be complete."

"*Gracias,*" Dad said. He immediately whizzed back down to the floor, dropped the cowering pig-man, and zoomed back up to his family.

When he arrived, his face was ashen.

"She's in the situation room!" he said.

That's when the whole family understood just how dire this crisis was.

The situation room was round and outfitted with a single titanium door. Inside were the most powerful defense mechanisms and sophisticated computer systems in existence. This room was where OSS leaders made enormous decisions. Where they enacted elaborate plans. Where they created strategies that saved the world on a daily basis.

And from this room, Dr. Hogg wanted to turn

all this good work on its ear. A sow's ear. She could, for instance, turn off all the electricity in Kansas City on a whim. She could make the Hoover dam dance the hokey pokey. She could force every TV station to play nothing but *Babe* and *Charlotte's Web.*

Nothing could stop her.

Which meant, for the Cortezes, intercepting Dr. Hogg had to happen now—or never.

"Off to the OSS?" Dad said.

Juni felt his stomach clench as they all nodded. He was feeling premature JJF-sickness already.

"I'll drive," he said wearily.

CHAPTER 14

A short while—and many bone-rattling bounces—later, the four Cortezes arrived at the OSS's headquarters. After grabbing some supplies, they clambered out of the big, round vehicle and crouched behind some shrubs. Juni reached into his spy bag.

"Juni!" Carmen said irritably. "This is no time for a snack. Do you, like, *ever* get full?"

Juni gave Carmen a dry glare. Then he pulled his hand out of his spy bag. He was holding Ralph the Second.

"Oh," Carmen said softly.

"I propose we send Ralph the Second on a reconnaissance run," Juni said. "He'll record everything he sees and hears. Then we'll know what we're up against."

"How many guards Dr. Hogg has posted," Mom said, nodding.

"What evil scheme Dr. Hogg has planned next," Dad said.

Juni gave Ralph the Second a little stroke on the head. He thought about the fate of Ralph the First—smashed in the line of duty on a recent mission. He shuddered. Then he set his jaw and said, "Go, Ralph."

The robot skittered away, and the Cortezes settled in to wait. After a moment of tense silence, Carmen spoke up.

"You know, Dad," she said, "it's really nice to know that, even if our lives are in peril and the safety of the world rests in our hands, that you're still enjoying yourself."

"What do you mean?" Dad said, looking at his daughter in confusion.

"You're wagging your tail!" Carmen hooted, pointing at her father's steadily swishing rear end.

"*Argh,*" Dad said, reaching back to grab his tail. "This is so humiliating."

"Oh, honey," Mom teased. "We know you love to save the world. Especially with your wife and kids. Wag away."

"You . . ." Dad growled irritably at Mom. But Juni could see there was a laughing glint in his dad's eyes. Even a . . . romantic glint.

"I know that look," Juni cried. "No kissing! We're on a mission."

"Er, of course," Mom said, looking regretful. "Mission first, kissing second."

"Yes, so we better get this over with quick!" Dad joked.

"Ugh," Juni said, rolling his eyes at his sister.

Suddenly, Juni heard a skittering sound.

"He's back!" Juni cried, just as Ralph the Second burst into the shrubs. He looked a little scuffed and trembly, but otherwise he was intact.

"Good work, robot!" Juni said, patting the contraption on its head. Then he punched a few buttons on Ralph's body. The little robot's head flipped over, revealing a tiny TV screen. Everything Ralph had recorded began to play on the screen. As the Cortezes watched, their hearts sank and their faces fell. Finally, Ralph's screen went blank.

"It's worse than I thought," Mom said darkly.

"Yeah," Juni said. "Dog-men and cat-women at every possible entrance to HQ."

"And Dr. Hogg *is* in the situation room," Carmen added, "but she's being guarded by dozens of croc-men."

"There's no way we can sneak past them," Dad said angrily.

Then the Cortezes gave each other hard looks.

"So, we fight them," Carmen declared. "They

may have numbers. And super strength. And, okay, lots of sharp teeth and claws . . ."

"And don't forget super spy training," Juni piped up.

"But we've got our wits," Carmen said.

"And one another," Mom added, giving her daughter a smile.

"Let's go," Dad said, hopping to his feet. "I think it's time for me and your mother to meet—Dr. Hogg."

A few minutes later, the Cortezes' plan was in place.

And it began with the furry super spies stationed at the OSS doors.

The spy family crept up to one of HQ's service entrances. According to Ralph the Second's intelligence, it was the most heavily guarded door to HQ. That's because it was the closest to the situation room, where Dr. Hogg was poised to commit who-knew-what kinds of fiendish crimes.

The Cortezes were definitely in for a tough fight.

Just before they reached the door, Dad paused and looked at the ground. His jaw clenched. Then he reached out to squeeze Juni by the shoulder.

"Big mission, son," Dad said.

"Yeah," Juni responded with a somber nod.

"I think this is as good a time as any to say, I want to give you something," Dad said.

As Dad spoke to Juni, Carmen shot Mom a smile. She remembered the warm mother-spy–daughter-spy exchange they'd had the day before. Now it was time for Dad and Juni to have their father-spy–son-spy moment.

"I want you to have . . ." Dad said quietly, "these."

Slowly, Dad held out his hand to Juni. Lying on his palm were two orange, puffy pellets.

"Wow, thanks, Dad!" Juni cried, giving his father a squeeze around the waist. "Uh . . . what are they?"

"Super spongy nose plugs!" Dad said. "Uncle Machete made them. You put them into your nose, you see? And when your dog and cat allergy makes your nose get all drippy and gross, the goo makes the nose plugs puff up! Your nose will be completely plugged. And your allergies will disappear!"

"Ew," Carmen muttered to her mom.

Juni happily inserted the puffy, orange things into his nose. He gave his father another hug.

"Thanks, Dad," he said. "I'm glad we had this little chat."

"Anytime, son," Dad said, ruffling Juni's hair. Or at least, what was left of it after the octopus's horrible haircut. Then Dad turned to Carmen.

"Are you ready, Carmenita?"

"Not quite yet," she said with a wink. She held out her hand. Dad slapped his hand on top of hers. Then Mom and Juni placed their hands on top. After a quick squeeze of solidarity, they broke apart.

"Now," Juni said, rolling up the sleeves of his OSS shirt. "We attack!"

CHAPTER 15

"**C**heep, cheep, cheep," Carmen called out. She waited. When nothing happened, she tried again: "Caw, caw, caw!"

Nothing.

She sighed.

"I feel really dumb!" she whispered.

"Well, I don't blame you," Juni whispered back to her.

Carmen was perched in a tree right outside the door to HQ. Juni and her parents were crouched at the tree's base. And for the past few minutes, Carmen had been singing every birdcall she knew.

"I don't understand," she whispered down to her parents. "I did the brown thrasher and the bluebird. The African hummingbird and even the tufted titmouse. They're not responding!"

"Well," Juni whispered, "you didn't try this!"

He threw back his head and screeched, "*Baaaaaaawk*-bawk-bawk-bawk-bawk-*BAAAAAWK*!"

The instant the last chicken squawk left his mouth, the HQ door flew open. First, a few whiskery noses peeked through the door. Then came a couple of sinuous paws.

"One more time," Carmen whispered.

"*BAAAAAWWWWK!*" Juni cried, making his parents wince and cover their ears.

"*Mrooowr!*"

A dozen cat-women suddenly bounded out of HQ.

And that's when Carmen took off.

Literally.

She had strapped to her arms one of Uncle Machete's latest gadgets—the Icarus II. The Icarus was a feathery pair of wings—giant wings. They extended ten feet beyond Carmen's fingertips. The lightest flapping of her arms made her zoom through the air.

"Whoo-hooooooo!" Carmen cried as she flew toward the clouds. "Oh, I mean, cheep, cheep, cheep!"

"*Mroooowr!*" the cat-women yowled. They began chasing after Carmen. She swooped toward the ground. But just when the cats were ready to pounce, she zoomed upward. She repeated this several times, teasing the cat-women into a frenzy.

Then, finally, she committed the *coup de grâce*. Carmen flew directly into a tall, bare-trunked tree. She sat on one of the branches—at least a hundred feet off the ground—and waited. She whistled and warbled as the cat-women streaked across the grass.

Just as Carmen had expected, the mutants flicked out their long, spiky nails and raced up the tree trunk, one feline after another. When the last cat-woman had scaled the tree, Carmen jumped out of it. Then she flapped her wings lightly, hovering just out of the mutants' reach.

"Cat up a tree without a fireman in sight," Carmen said. "Too bad, ladies!"

The cat-women gaped at Carmen.

Then they gazed at the distant ground.

And then, they began yowling pitifully.

They were stuck.

What's more, they were out of the Cortezes' way. Which left only the dog-men.

Juni knew what no dog could resist. Precisely because it was the same thing *he* couldn't resist—food! And he just happened to have a bag filled with smooshed-up cheeseburgers, PB & J sandwiches, and French fries—*just* the sort of table scraps that dogs yearned for.

As Carmen landed near her parents, Juni moseyed up to the HQ door. The dog-men peeked out at him. They began baring their spiky teeth and growling. But before they could pounce, Juni tossed the contents of his bag out into the OSS grounds. The pack went bounding after the food, howling with doggy desire.

Every dog-man was taken care of—except one.

And this one stayed behind. He was really more of a puppy-boy than a dog-man. He had soft, floppy ears and a whiskery face, and he panted winningly. He gazed at Juni with sad, brown eyes.

He whimpered pathetically.

And he looked very, very lonely.

"Uh, hey, boy," Juni said hesitantly. "Go get the food. Go on!"

But the puppy-boy stayed put.

As Carmen watched this—sort of cute—mutant, she began to get nervous. Juni's nose plugs were completely squelching his allergies. This was his one opportunity to play with a dog! And was there any force more powerful than a boy and his dog?

Perhaps Juni would be taken in by this puppy-boy's con job.

Perhaps he'd forget his mission entirely and go off for a romp with the mutant!

If he did, all was lost.

Carmen and her parents held their breath as Juni reached into his spy vest pocket. He pulled out a little red ball. "Want to play?" Juni asked the puppy-boy.

Oh, no! Carmen thought. Juni's gonna blow it.

Just as the thought flashed through Carmen's mind, Juni glanced over his shoulder.

"I know what you're thinking, Carmen," he said. "And all I have to say is, 'Am not!'"

Then he turned back to the puppy-boy and yelled, "Fetch!"

He threw the ball away from the OSS with all his strength. The little mutant gave a yelp and began racing after the ball. Which meant the OSS's entrance was completely clear.

"Come on!" Juni yelled to his family. In two shakes, they'd all tumbled into the building and barred the door with one of Uncle Machete's Insta-Wardrobes. (This was a heavy, fist-sized gadget. Pull a ripcord in the gizmo, and it turned into a giant, very heavy, six-drawer dresser, which could be pushed up against a door to form an instant blockade.)

"On to the situation room!" Carmen said.

"And the croc-men," Dad said. "Everybody got their sticks ready?"

"Ready!" the rest of the family cried. They each pulled a bundle of long sticks—which they'd collected from the OSS grounds earlier—out of their spy bags. Then they ran down the short corridor to the situation room.

And sure enough, there were hordes of croc-men waiting for them. At least a dozen of them guarded the locked titanium door.

When they saw the Cortezes, they immediately lunged at them, snapping their long jaws loudly.

But the spy family was unfazed. In fact, they seemed to welcome the attack!

"Ticktock, ticktock," Juni taunted one of the croc-men. "Come and get me!"

The instant the croc-man attacked, Juni thrust his thick tree branch into the mutant's gaping mouth. The stick became wedged just behind the villain's front teeth. It held! And since the stick was too far away for the croc-man to reach with his short, burly arms, his mouth stayed propped open. He was completely powerless!

While Juni took out that croc-man, his family got busy with the others.

Carmen used her gymnastic skills to bob and weave among the scaly mutants, planting her sticks in their mouths so fast, they barely saw her.

And Mom and Dad sashayed their way to success.

"Care to dance?" Dad asked Mom with a little bow.

"Tango?" Mom replied slyly.

"But, of course," Dad said, slipping his arm around his wife's waist.

Together, they stalked toward a croc-man, their arms outstretched. Without breaking their stride, they thrust a stick into the villain's mouth.

Then Dad spun Mom around. Along the way, she took out four more croc-men that had encircled them.

And, to cap off the dance, Dad sent Mom into a deep dip. He lowered her to the floor, where she was perfectly poised to thrust a stick into the mouth of a final croc-man, who'd been crawling stealthily toward them.

When Mom whipped up from the dip, Carmen and Juni applauded.

"We got them all!" Juni cried. He shook his fist as the traumatized croc-men ran away from the situation room in terror. Their mouths were still propped painfully open.

"Thanks for the dance," Mom said to Dad, dropping into a curtsy.

"Ah, but now we face the belle of the ball," Dad said. "Helga S.A. Hogg. Carmen?"

"I'm way ahead of you," Carmen said. She was standing before the enormous titanium door. Pulling a stethoscope out of her cargo pants pocket, she listened to the door. Then she began typing into its computerized lock.

Finally, her highly trained ears picked up the precise click she'd been waiting for. Whipping the stethoscope out of her ears, she looked at her family.

"I'm in," she announced.

"Let's do this," Juni said, squinting at the door. He grabbed the handle and pulled. The door swung open with a mighty creak and a long hiss.

With their fists in the air, the four Cortezes leaped into the situation room.

Dr. Hogg was waiting for them.

She was standing on the conference room table. And she was holding a sparking, ominous, and very large weapon.

"Ah, hello," she oinked. "I've been expecting you."

"You have?" Juni blurted.

"Of course," Dr. Hogg snorted. "You're the Cortezes. The best spies in the OSS. I knew you wouldn't go down without a fight."

"You got that right, Hogg," Carmen said.

"That's why I'm prepared," Dr. Hogg said. "Ingrid, Gregorio, remember the metal skullcaps that turned you into those very cute puppies?"

"What about them?" Dad barked. His tail flailed angrily.

"Antiques!" Dr. Hogg declared. "All that cumbersome lab equipment—it was such a pain. That's why I invented *this* beauty."

She held up her sparking gun.

"An animalizing ray gun," Dr. Hogg cackled. "Hot off the presses."

She pointed the gun at Juni and pulled the trigger! A giant zotz of lightning shot out of the weapon, hitting Juni right in the belly!

CHAPTER 16

"Juni!" Mom and Carmen screamed. Dr. Hogg's animalizing ray had surrounded Juni with a puff of smoke. They couldn't see him at all.

Dad didn't hesitate for a moment. He leaped at Dr. Hogg with one, powerful jump. But before he could grab her, Dr. Hogg turned the ray gun on him!

Zottttz!

The blast stopped Dad in midair. He crashed to the ground in another puff of smoke.

Mom and Carmen began coughing and waving the smoke clouds out of their eyes. When the fog finally cleared, the female spies stared.

Juni and Dad were gone.

In Dad's place was a baboon—long blue nose, embarrassingly rosy backside and all!

"At least, the dog tail's gone," Carmen said to her Mom in a shaky voice. "Now where's Juni?!"

Eeeeeeep! Ahh-choo!

Carmen followed the screech until she spotted a little, curly-tailed monkey in the corner! Juni had become a monkey! Which meant he was now allergic to himself! His sneeze made his orange super-puffy nose plugs shoot out of his nostrils. They landed wetly on Dr. Hogg's arm.

"Oink!" Dr. Hogg screamed in disgust. She shook her plump arm so hard, she lost her balance and careened off the conference table. Carmen heard her land with a fleshy *splat*.

That gave Carmen and Mom time to dive to either side of the situation room and crouch behind a couple of wide-backed chairs.

Okay, Carmen thought desperately. If Mom and I get zapped by the animalizing ray, we're doomed. We have to overpower Dr. Hogg. And to do that, we're going to have to work together.

Carmen peeked over her chair back. Beyond her chittering monkey-brother and chest-thumping baboon-father, she saw her mother's determined green eyes gazing back at her.

And suddenly, a feeling of peace—and power—surged through Carmen. She knew that together, as daughter-spy and mother-spy, she and her mom would conquer Helga S.A. Hogg.

The question was—how?

"Oooh," Carmen muttered to herself, "if I could just get my hands on that animalizing ray gun, I know I could cross-wire it. . . ."

Before she could even finish her thought, her Mom was putting that very plan into action. She popped up from behind her chair and whooped, "Suuuuu-*ey!*"

"Oink?" Dr. Hogg's head jolted up from behind the conference table. She still looked a little wobbly. But she was also half pig. That meant she was powerless to resist Mom's expert hog call.

Once she had Dr. Hogg's attention, Mom reached into her pants pocket. She pulled out something small.

And round.

And dusty.

"Want a truffle?" Mom shouted.

"*Oink!*" Dr. Hogg snorted excitedly. She climbed awkwardly onto the conference table, dragging her ray gun with her. But when Mom whipped the truffle across the room, Dr. Hogg squealed. She dropped her ray gun and leaped off the table. She galumphed behind the conference room whiteboard and began snuffling frantically in search of the truffle.

"Great minds think alike!" Carmen exclaimed.

She dashed to the table and snatched up the ray gun. She squinted at it.

"It's a 20,000-megahertz quaditron," she said, biting her lip. "This is going to take a few seconds."

Just as she began dissecting the ray gun's wiring, Carmen was startled by a high-pitched *eeeeeeeep!* It was the monkey—er, Juni! Dad the baboon was howling, too.

Carmen glanced up and saw Dr. Hogg licking her snout and making delighted grunting noises. Clearly, she'd located the truffle. And devoured it. And now, for the main course, she was going for—her mother!

"Don't worry about me, Carmen," Mom shouted. "I'll handle the Hogg."

Carmen resumed her work while her Mom dropped into a fighting stance.

"I learned a new martial art when I was in Brazil," Carmen heard Mom say. "It's called Mon Kae Si, Mon Kae Du."

"What?" Carmen cried. She looked up from the ray gun again. "Mom! Don't use it. It's totally bogus. The mutants made it up to distract us."

"I know," Mom said as she launched into a handstand. "So I made a few alterations. Now I'm calling it *Mom* Kae Si, *Mom* Kae Du."

With that, Mom wrapped her ankles around Dr. Hogg's snout. Then she flicked her toes lightly— and sent the evil veterinarian flying.

"*Eeeeeeeep,*" Juni cheered. "*Ah-chooo!*"

"*Ooof, oof, oof,*" Dad echoed.

Breathing hard, Carmen turned back to the ray gun. She crisscrossed two essential wires, then whipped her mini-soldering iron out of her utility belt and fired it up. She inserted the tiny flame into the ray gun and watched the sparks fly. When she had finished, she eyed the ray gun's innards.

"Well, it's messy," she said, "but it should work."

She picked up the ray gun and squinted through its eyepiece.

Then she huffed in frustration and lowered the gun.

Dr. Hogg and her mother were entangled in combat. Dr. Hogg had Mom by the waist. Mom's arm was clenched around Hogg's neck. And their feet were so tangled up, Carmen could barely tell Mom's toes from Hogg's trotters.

"I can't get a clean shot of Dr. Hogg, Mom!" she called out.

"I . . . can't . . . break free," Mom replied through gritted teeth.

"*Grrrrrrrrr.*"

"Who's that?" Carmen cried in alarm. She looked wildly around the situation room. The monkey-Juni was swinging his tiny fists and jumping up and down on top of the whiteboard.

It was Baboon-Dad who was the source of that ominous, angry growl.

He was baring long, sharp teeth.

And he was glaring at Dr. Hogg.

Then he turned away from the super villain for a moment to look straight at Carmen. He nodded his simian snout.

Carmen nodded. She knew what Dad wanted her to do.

Dad turned back to Dr. Hogg—and pounced! He landed on the evil mutant's back and dug his teeth into her shirt collar. Then he yanked with all his strength.

"Aaaargh," Dr. Hogg rasped as her OSS fatigues pulled at her neck. Finally, she released her grip on Mom and grabbed for her collar. As Mom stumbled away, Dad yanked Dr. Hogg off her feet. The pig-woman and the baboon landed in an entangled heap.

Carmen squinted one eye shut.

She took careful aim.

And then she pulled the animalizing ray gun's trigger.

Zoooootttz!

The blast sent a blue flash through the air. Once again, an opaque cloud of smoke filled the room. Once again, Carmen and her mother hacked and coughed.

And when the smoke cleared, there was Carmen's father—fully human *and* tail-less, to boot! He was clutching a big, ugly, squealing sow. Helga S.A. Hogg really was a hog now! The only crime she'd be capable of after this was terrorizing a barnyard.

"Yay!" Carmen squealed, leaping off the conference table and into her parents' embrace. She was so happy that, for a moment, she forgot all about Juni.

"Eeeeeepp!" the monkey-Juni shrieked. Dad started as the little animal hopped off the whiteboard and landed on his shoulder. Dad looked at Mom and Carmen.

"Juni?" he asked.

"Juni," they confirmed.

"It'll be okay, son," Dad said. He put the trembling monkey onto the table. Then he looked at Carmen and nodded.

"You can give him a zap now, honey," Dad said.

"Okay," Carmen said. But then, she hesitated.

"You know," she mused, "a monkey would make an excellent pet. Maybe we should just *keep* Juni like this."

"EEEEEEEPPPP!" the monkey squealed. He hopped up and down and shook his tiny fists. Then he sneezed.

"Carmen . . ." Mom said.

"Oh, all right," Carmen said with a grin. Then she aimed the ray gun at her little brother and pulled the trigger.

Zotz!

CHAPTER 17

"I think we should call you Squeakums," Juni said.

He was sitting on the exercise mat in the basement training room of the Cortez mansion. And he was addressing a little, black-and-white-speckled bunny. The rabbit hopped into Juni's arms and squeaked sweetly. Then he began nuzzling Juni's face.

"Hey, watch it," Juni laughed. "Knock out my super puffy nose plugs and I'll be allergic to you, Squeakums."

Squeak!

"Yeah," Juni giggled. Then he started cooing in baby talk. "That's the pewfect name for you! Because you are so cute and squeaky. Aren't you, wittle guy? Aren't you!"

"Squeakums, huh?"

Juni jumped and glanced over his shoulder. Carmen was standing on the bottom step of the basement stairs. And she was smirking at him.

"How much of that did you hear?" Juni shouted.

"All of it," Carmen laughed. "And I bet I know some Spy Kids in the OSS who would love to hear all about it."

"No!" Juni roared.

"What's it worth to ya?" Carmen asked.

Juni heaved a big sigh. "Okay," he grumbled. "You get to name the rabbit."

"Ha!" Carmen said. She sat down next to Juni and gathered their new pet in her arms.

"I can't believe it's only been two days since we found this guy hopping around the grounds of the OSS!" Carmen said.

"Yeah, right after the police hauled Helga S.A. Hogg off to a petting zoo," Juni said.

"And we turned all the mutants back into OSS agents," Carmen said. She patted the bunny idly. "So, everything turned out all right in the end. *And* we got a pet. A pet that *I* get to name."

She let the adorable bunny hop across the exercise mat. Then she put her finger to her chin and thought hard.

"Let's see, bunny," she said. "I think I'll name you . . ."

"Carmen!"

Carmen jumped and looked up. Mom and Dad were both standing at the foot of the stairs. They looked somber. Almost sinister.

And Dad was holding—a weapon.

"Uh, Dad?" Juni said in a quavering voice. "What are you doing?"

"What I must," Dad said grimly. He raised the weapon to his shoulder and aimed it—at their bunny!

"Dad, no!" Carmen begged. "He's so cute!"

"We promised we'd take good care of him," Juni cried. "Please, don't shoot!"

Dad shot.

Zotz!

A blue bolt zinged out of the ray gun and hit the bunny right between his floppy ears. He uttered one feeble squeak. Then the rabbit was surrounded by a poof of smoke.

With sinking hearts, Carmen and Juni waited for the smoke to clear. When it did, a grown man was sitting on the exercise mat. He was twitching his nose and had his hands curled up beneath his clefted chin.

"Mr. Devlin!" Carmen and Juni cried.

"Yes, children," Mom said, striding across the mat to help Devlin to his feet. "Ever since we completed our mission, you've been keeping our boss as a pet!"

"Uh, sorry, Mr. Devlin," Carmen said sheepishly. "We didn't know."

"Uh-huh," Devlin said sternly. "You didn't even *wonder* what Helga Hogg had done with me?"

"Well, you were so cute!" Juni cried. "It didn't even occur to us that—"

"Cute, huh?" Devlin said. "Squeakums, huh?"

Juni turned beet red and hung his head.

"Listen, Spy Kids," Devlin said gruffly, "run to the kitchen and get me a couple carrots, and we'll be even."

Carmen and Juni sighed with relief and headed for the stairs.

"Oh, and kids . . ." Devlin called after them.

"Yes, sir?" the Spy Kids said. They paused to look back at the OSS chief. He flashed them a rakish smile and a thumbs-up.

"Thanks for saving the world," he said. "Again."

Carmen and Juni grinned at their boss. Their parents grinned proudly at *them.* And then the Spy Kids headed to the kitchen.

"So," Juni said as he opened the fridge to look for some carrots. "Not only have we rid the world of all those half-beast super spies, we've also lost Squeakums. What kind of pet do you think we should get?"

Carmen leaned against the kitchen counter and thought for a moment. Then she said, "How about . . . a goldfish?"

Juni's face lit up.

"Yeah," he agreed. "A nice *peaceful* goldfish. Sounds perfect!"